Is There Anybody to Love You?

Kalin Terziyski

IS THERE ANYBODY
TO LOVE YOU?

Translated from Bulgarian by David Mossop

DALKEY ARCHIVE PRESS

Originally published in Bulgarian by Janet 45 Publishers (Bulgaria) as *Ima li koy da vi obicha* in 2009.

Library of Congress Cataloging-in-Publication Data
Names: Terziyski, Kalin author. | Mossop, David, translator.
Title: Is there anybody to love you? / Kalin Terziyski ; translated from the Bulgarian by David Mossop.
Other titles: Ima li koy da vi obicha. English
Description: First Dalkey Archive edition. | McLean, IL : Dalkey Archive Press, 2018.
Identifiers: LCCN 2018026046 | ISBN 9781628972740 (pbk. : alk. paper)
Classification: LCC PG1039.3.E79 I4313 2018 | DDC 891.73/5--dc23
LC record available at https://lccn.loc.gov/2018026046

Co-funded by the Creative Europe Programme of the European Union

www.dalkeyarchive.com
McLean, IL / Dublin

The European Commission support for the production of this publication does not constitute an endorsement of the contents which reflects the views only of the author, and the commission cannot be held responsible for any use which may be made of the information contained therein.

Contents

Is There Anybody to Love You?

IT IS RAINING outside, getting on toward evening and water's gushing out of the drainpipes on the balconies. There's a woman in the street screaming ugly, incomprehensible words. In the summer evenings the streets give off a different, special sort of noise. The rain is refreshing the air, but there's nothing else really happening. I'm with E.J. We're sitting in the office where we work. I don't actually know what I do at work.

There seem to be a lot of people hanging around the office doing something. I'm the same. I usually just sit here playing computer games waiting while someone finishes what they're doing, so that I can get on with it after them. I suppose I'm like a cleaner or supervisor on a building site. Actually I'm a doctor. E.J. and I are both doctors. We both became disillusioned with medicine at the same time. Not medicine in general, but what we call medicine in Bulgaria. There's too much filth in what we call medicine in Bulgaria. At the moment we're sitting in the office doing nothing. We're drinking beer. Better than nothing.

When I think about offices, I imagine the closets where school janitors keep the buckets, brooms, and mops they use to clean the toilets.

We're sitting drinking beer and talking about insignificant things. If we could talk about significant things, we probably would.

E.J. walks back and forth, drumming his fingers on the objects around him.

3

"I saw Martin K. last night," E.J. says. I spin around on my chair and ask him:

"Was he depressed?"

"No. He was drunk. Actually both . . . a bit depressed and very drunk."

Martin K. is a well-known journalist and media pundit, and he's our friend. We've womanized and drunk alcohol together and spent the last ten years talking about life. But recently he's been in a really weird psychological state. He's become irritable, argumentative about petty things, and depressed.

"He called me last night and said he needed me," E.J. says. Martin K. called me yesterday as well. He asked me to go to the airport with him to see off Lily Marlene Hummer Longlegs. I asked him, "Why?" And he said, "I need you. I want to shout and sing until the plane takes off." "I'm not going to shout . . . that's stupid . . . I'm too tired for that sort of thing. You're talking nonsense. Go and see her off by yourself. Bye."

A few hours later Martin K. called me again and said, "I need you." "No, no. I'm too tired. Have you seen her off?" "Yes. But I don't want to talk about that. I need to have someone with me." "Have a drink and you'll feel better," I replied, and I made a move to put the phone down so that I could watch the rest of the stupid film I was pointlessly filling my evening with.

Martin K. shouted out in a vulgar drunken voice: "You're a miserable queer! A talentless, stupid, idiot and a pathetic, miserable queer!" And he put the phone down. Clearly he wasn't feeling well.

I have to tell you who Lily Marlene Hummer Longlegs is. We met her about ten years ago, at the seaside, when she was still a little girl.

Now she's a pretty, tall, dark-skinned woman with an Egyptian beauty. She has white teeth and black hair and a strange mark on her upper lip. She's a bright, kind girl. She's a little arrogant, but just enough to prove she's not just a tart from Liulin working in a video studio.

She lives in the USA with some Italian. He works for the World Bank. I've got no idea what the World Bank is, but then why should I have to know about all the wonderful places where people are legally fleeced?

When I heard she was living with an Italian, it seemed strangely perverse. It gave me an acid stomach. The very word "Italian" makes me think of homosexual encounters in men's restrooms, eating frogs and pasta. I think I must have watched too many cheap films.

Lily Marlene Longlegs came back to Bulgaria after a five-year absence and immediately called Martin K. I don't know if she had been particularly interested in him before that. I actually have no idea how Martin K. manages to attract women. He hypnotizes them like a python. They're rodents and he's the python.

She called him from the airport and they met even before she went to see her parents.

For weeks Martin K. went around as nervous as a pedigree pointer, excitedly telling everyone how good she is at blow jobs, and what she says in English when she's giving them. Her World Bank English, special phrases for blow jobs. He told everyone how much he loved her for shouting out in English and all the rest of it. How much he wanted to marry her, to be her bodyguard, her servant, gigolo, how he wanted to beat the fuck out of the Italian and all other Italians.

He talked about her as if he was really in love. He took her to restaurants, spent money on her, got drunk, and asked her to marry him.

A week later she had to go to the hospital to have a stent inserted into her renal artery. It was cheaper to have it done in Bulgaria, and the filthy Italian wouldn't stump up the money to have it done in the USA!

Martin K. serenaded her at the hospital. He sang silly songs beneath the window of her hospital room.

Perhaps she really did love him, I said to myself that same evening when he serenaded her. And perhaps he really loved her.

Then, yesterday actually, she went back to America to give her skinflint Italian blow jobs while shouting in English. Perhaps she wanted to make sure the World Bank wasn't slacking off in its attempts to fleece people.

Now Martin K. was sitting by himself getting drunk from grief and emptiness. These are all things I know about.

Five years ago, or was it seven, we used to drink beer and talk about the same things we do now. The same old friends. We talked about love and women, women and blow jobs. Our whole life has passed in talking about the same old things. A strange generation of losers who don't want to do anything important in their lives. I might be wrong. The world is full of thirty-year-old men and women employed in PR, management, and other such crap, who dress smartly and work twelve hours a day.

In the World Bank for example. I suppose they must be the real people of this generation. We don't envy them. If there's something we're envious of, then it's the confidence they have that they'll get out of bed again tomorrow and work for twelve hours or more, and their even greater confidence that this makes them so much more important than any run-of-the-mill assholes.

We're sitting and talking as it rains. The rain makes the air fresh. I feel tense. Sometimes even the most experienced parasites get a feeling of unease—there's a good Turkish word, *saclet*, which encapsulates this feverish sense of guilt for doing absolutely nothing. I sit down in front of my computer and make a suggestion to E.J.

"Why don't we write something . . ."

E.J. looks at me through his concave mongoloid eyes and with a mocking sing-song voice starts dictating:

"Anna Karenina, rhubarb, rhubarb, Turkish custard, give me five levs . . ."

I say, "We have to write something, otherwise what's the point of just sitting here?"

E.J. paces up and down the office, humming a tune and kicking the chairs: "I've got no idea what the point is of just sitting here. I don't even know the point of why I'm alive . . ."

E.J. and I, and Martin K. as well, are writers. It's a good way to justify doing nothing, showing off in front of women, and explaining why you've got a chronic hangover while earning enough money to get another one.

Martin K. is a serious writer, we're not very . . . He takes things seriously, he drinks seriously and sleeps seriously with all the women who come within a hundred yards of him. Now he's suffering seriously.

We have to write. We can't just sit here doing nothing.

Ever since the great Douglas Adams started using a word processor, writing has become a job for technocrats. Shift, insert, format, undo, and so on, and so on. We're not even semi-technocrats, we don't like writing. That's why we're writers. Nobody really likes writing these days, and nobody really likes working. It's a sad fact, no two ways about it. How is it that all these young studs who work twelve hours a day are so wonderfully confident? They're confident that tomorrow when they wake up, they will be welcomed with open arms into a Heaven where yuppies can work eighteen hours every day. Writing is a job for self-sufficient people who live in caves, eat fungus, and once every month go to international conferences to campaign against AIDS or something.

I look down at the floor, drink some beer, and say to E.J.:

"So what do you want to do, you miserable loser, if you don't want to write? Why don't you want to write?"

"I don't want to write. I want to womanize. That's what I want to do. I'm not a writer, I'm a womanizer."

Actually that's not true. E.J. has a particular attitude toward women. In fact all of us idle poets have a particular attitude toward women. For example, if I read somewhere something like, "they threw themselves at each other and began to have wild, untamed, animal sex," it makes me feel sick. I get short of breath and exhausted. Why, I ask myself, have people been trying for tens of thousands of years to achieve the heights of civilization, just to enjoy the wild and bestial things in life? Isn't it better just to lie still in your cool bedroom while a calm and wise woman sucks on your penis quietly and profoundly? That's what I think, and that's what E.J. thinks as well. Wild, aggressive, volcanic sex was invented so that healthy, thinking business people could relax after work. It strengthens the arteries. These same healthy, thinking business shitheads have sex in the same way they do everything else. They have sex. They have children. They make money. They make love and not war, but when they have to, they make war. They drink juice, freshly squeezed juice. They run, they lift weights. They swim, they surf, they go here and there, drive their cars, talk about them. They have three children, they have aims, jobs to do, they fuck the shit out of everybody, and they expect gratitude for it, and so on.

E.J. and I, we look at things in a different way.

E.J. says, "I don't want to get laid, I just want to go somewhere with some friends and some women, just for pleasure. Just for the sake of it, for the freedom of it."

E.J. has always liked to talk to his friends and he likes women to listen to him. Every man likes to talk to his friends about art, cars, military service, and women, and they like women to listen.

I like E.J.'s views on life because they are similar to mine.

E.J.: "Women are just for luxury."

Are women really luxury? I wonder. I think about Lily Marlene Hummer Longlegs. Yes, she's a luxury woman. She's not the sort of woman to help you clean out the cellar. She won't carry boxes full of mouse shit and fluff out of your filthy cellar. She won't even help you clean your soul.

What is Martin K. doing? He's probably trying not to feel empty and alone. Is he drinking or working?

He might be watching a TV show about animals. I've noticed that people watch lots of shows about animals when they feel empty and alone.

Should I call him? It's better not to call someone when they're feeling bad. You just burden him with the demand to behave normally. Isn't that right?

E.J. spits out of the window as if he can tell I'm thinking about Martin K.

"Yesterday, you know, my dad, you know, he likes reading in the toilet, all the books he's read in recent years, he's read them there, well, he went into the toilet with *Defloration*.

Defloration was Martin K.'s first book, a slim volume of poetry. Some of the poems are good, some are naive, but on the whole it's a good book. Most of the poems are dirty.

E.J. continues:

"So he sat there in the toilet for more than half an hour reading Martin K.'s *Defloration*. When he came out, he asked me, 'Who wrote this crap?' 'No, Dad, it wasn't me,' I said. And then I got scared that he wouldn't leave me his apartment in his will, all because of Martin K.'s stupid fucking poetry."

That's it! I say to myself. That's the sort of thing that interests adults: wars and funerals, radiotherapy and the hole in the ozone layer. When they start talking about the organs men and women use to make little children, it makes them hypocritically vomit and spit. I suppose I must be an adult. I've got a grown-up kid. Perhaps that's where it all comes from, I think to myself. Nobody can ever believe that one day their child will have sex.

Martin K. has his own show on Darik Radio. It's very sharp and very witty, at least that's what the women he fucks say. Actually it's what I think as well. He's on the radio tonight. He'll be live on air in a couple of hours' time.

"Do you know the subject of Martin's show tonight?" I ask E.J.

He clatters pointlessly on the computer keyboard.

"Is there anybody to love you? That's his subject tonight," E.J. answers. "Why don't we call him and pretend to be someone else, different people every five minutes, and tell him, 'Nobody loves you, asshole.' Or we could pretend to be Italian and say, '*Buongiorno*, Signor Martin, have you by any chance fucked my girlfriend?'"

"That's a bit over the top, isn't it?"

"Not at all," E.J. replies.

"Actually it's quite an interesting subject. 'Is there anybody to love you?' Mommy, Daddy, the woman you're with, the woman you just slept with, your friends, your children, and God knows who. Is there really anybody to love you? I've thought about it at times, and if I think for long enough, I start crying."

"Why don't we call Martin K. and tell him the names of everyone who loves him?" I ask E.J.

"Why should we lie to him? If someone called you and told you something like that, would you believe him?"

E.J.'s right. It's easy enough to believe it when someone says they hate us, but it's very difficult to believe it when they say they love us. I don't believe women who say they love me. I used to want to believe them, but I know now that when they're young it's their sex hormones talking garbage. Then as the years pass, they say they love us out of fear and loneliness. I'm scared even my child doesn't love me. Even when she does say it, I suspect it's because she wants to get her own way. How rotten is that!

What is Martin K. doing while he's preparing for his show about "Is there anybody to love you?"

E.J. told me that as she was leaving, Lily Marlene Longlegs said all sorts of things to Martin K. She told him that she was actually unhappy in America, lonely, very lonely, and couldn't love anybody else, but that she had to go back to America, because her life sucked and it wasn't up to her. Oh yes, life sucks and nothing's up to us. She told him that she would think about him all the time. He asked her: "Even when you're fucking your Italian?" She was taken aback by his vulgarity and started crying: "Yes, even then."

Then Martin K. turned around and left, trying to look hard, trying not to show his emotions and not allow a single tear to escape from the corner of his eye to erode his arrogance. Like Hemingway, who never got upset when he parted from his countless lovers. I know, however, that it hit him very hard. He said to himself that she really had fucked him over, but he wasn't really angry, he was just feeling empty and sad.

Outside the rain is slowly stopping. It's a wet summer's night and completely dark. There's a woman in the street screaming ugly and incomprehensible words. In the summertime the noise in the streets is worrying. Nothing's happening, the rain has stopped but the air is no fresher.

E.J. and I are sitting in the office where I work. Though *work* is a strong word. Why pretend? We're sitting talking about who loves Martin K. Each of us is probably thinking about who could love himself. We're so lazy and so insensitive, so protected against grief by boredom, that we don't feel anything while we're talking.

I turn on the radio to listen to Martin K.'s show about "Is there anybody to love you?" The theme song plays out and then his normal confident voice, but not as confident as usual, says: "Hello, night owls of Sofia, you're listening to Darik Radio and I'm Martin K. Today, we're going to talk about something unusual. You might be used to me talking about prostitutes, gay marriage, and rare venereal diseases. You're probably expecting me to talk about soft and hard drugs, or ask when was the first time you tried anal sex. This evening, however, I've decided for purely personal reasons to talk about something else. This evening's subject is 'Is there anybody to love you?' A slightly unusual subject. I've decided to do something a little bit different this evening. I'm not going to ask questions. I'll just leave the telephone line open and anybody who wants to can just call and talk. I've also told my producer, or rather, asked her, not to intrude and let the calls straight through without worrying about me. There's nothing to worry about, I won't say anything. I don't want to do the talking this evening. Anybody can call and say live, on-air, if they have anybody who loves them. For my sake, please list everyone who loves you. That's all I have to say, apart from good-bye. Call the studio telephones and say loud and clear who loves you. Here we go."

Then the radio emits a loud crack. It sounds very much like a gunshot. It is a gunshot. For the next five minutes there's silence. Then the first listener comes on air to list everyone who loves him.

E.J. and I just stand there not knowing what to do.

The Collector of Valuable Things

THE COLLECTOR OF valuable things takes a crushed pack of cigarettes out of his pocket. This is one of the valuable things he owns. He lights a cigarette using a cigarette lighter with a faded picture of a naked lady on it. This is another of his valuable things. He sniffs and spits as he drags his half-filled grocery cart of valuable things. He walks slowly along the street. It's an old street and the buildings arranged along either side are dark gray. The collector looks distracted, but this is because his eyes are half-closed from the cigarette smoke. He normally stares closely at the ground in front of him so as not to miss anything. His gaze falls upon something which might be interesting. It's a piece of pleasantly yellow paper. He bends down and picks up a page of a newspaper. It's stuck between a garbage bin and a deserted newspaper stand and must have been there for a whole year while it yellowed. Yes, the date shows that it's from exactly a year ago. The headline reads: "Capricorn—March will be a good month for business, Aries—a good month for love." There are obituaries on the other side. One of the photographs is of a pretty young girl with intelligent eyes. "That's valuable," the collector thinks and stuffs the sheet of paper between the other valuable things in his cart. He continues along the street, inspired by the abundance of valuable things which the streets, pavements, garbage bins and the World have to offer. He finds a leg from a Barbie doll, an empty perfume bottle which still smells nice, a pen with an empty cartridge, the head of a still-fresh carnation, a magpie's feather, the second half of Leo Tolstoy's *Kreutzer*

Sonata, a teaspoon and a printed circuit board from some electronic device. He puts it in a convenient place in his cart, so he can find it later. He's pleased with what he's found and now examines the ground in front of him with an expression of satisfaction. He's collected enough valuable things for the day. He sets off for home. When he gets there, he carefully carries the cart up the stairs to the second floor and enters his kingdom of valuable things. To anybody else it's a pigsty, a dump filled with revolting garbage, the stuff of nightmares! But for the collector of valuable things, it is the most fantastic place in the world. It is home to the remnants of human happiness, sadness, pleasure, work, desperation, brilliance, fear, stupidity, drunkenness, and madness. The collector of valuable things looks around his estate with an air of satisfaction. He spends a whole hour arranging his newly acquired things. Then he sits down on the floor, lights a cigarette, and reads one of the love letters he found ten or so days ago, tied in a bundle and cautiously thrown into the bushes near the canal. The letter begins like this:

My darling, my darling, my darling, I haven't touched you for three whole days, I haven't kissed you, I haven't heard your voice and I haven't touched your hair. I miss you so much that it is like physical pain, as if a vital organ has been removed from my body. Even the air I breathe without you is tasteless and not enough to fill my lungs. The whole world is empty without you . . .

That's valuable, the collector of valuable things thinks to himself, and he puts the stub of the cigarette he has just extinguished in a suitable place and lights another one.

The Beggar

I AM WALKING along Ivan Asen Street with my daughter, looking at the houses. The houses in Sofia are ugly because they're old. Their age doesn't do anything to enhance their beauty, just destroys their rendering.

I see a couple of women, but they have wide hips, narrow shoulders, and look deliberately sexual. They look as if they want something bad, right here and right now. They have a deliberate plan to marry rich men and bear male children who will become good soldiers and kill some innocent little person while he's having lunch.

So I carry on walking and look at everything as if it's nothing. This is quite hard to do, even though everyone does it subconsciously every day.

"Do you want some pizza?"

"Mmmm, yes . . . ," my daughter drawls.

It annoys me to no end when she tilts her head to the side with that distracted, girlish, entranced look on her face. Her head in the clouds. But I'm no different. She looks on everything as if it's nothing.

"But you'll eat it, if we get some, won't you?" I ask her, tugging her arm.

"Mmmm, yes . . . ," she replies, continuing to look into the invisible beyond, still distracted.

I know all about distraction. It's when you don't think, don't feel, don't see and don't hear. You just live. It's an easy way of attaining a childish Nirvana.

We walk toward the stand where they sell pizzas. I take care we don't get hit by a car. My daughter limply holds onto my hand. She stumbles lightly against my legs, because she's not looking where she's going.

While I take care not to get hit by a car, I think about my childhood. Did I feel good all the time during my childhood? Did I actually feel anything at all? Did I constantly feel that mixture of guilt and irritation at the constant list of things I was always forced to do? Of course not. That's the sort of thing I've felt since I became an adult. As a child I probably felt childish nonsense.

My daughter is suddenly startled by a big dog that darts out in front of us. I'm completely distracted.

"Look where you're going. I thought you were supposed to be the adult." She tugs my arm.

"Yes, I'm an adult." It's so sad. But I think I was sadder when I was a child. I fully understood that I was dependent on everything and everyone, and that all the real pleasures of life were hidden from me. My mother was very strict and kept the wardrobe locked. One day I found the key. Apart from a few unopened bottles of poor-quality champagne left over from a stupid New Year's party, and stacks of folded clothes that smelled like mothballs, I found a box of tampons. I was both shocked and excited by my discovery. It was both disgusting and enticing at the same time, but hidden from me. I didn't really understand what those little cylinders were for, but I felt intuitively that they went in somewhere, and that somewhere was the temple of my shameful and secret religion.

I think that I decided to grow up just to shake off my childhood.

"*Tatesh* . . ." (I have no idea why my daughter invented that Hungarian name for me.) "We're here. What are you thinking about?"

"Nothing, your dad's head's always full of nonsense."

We go in and I take a quick but annoyed look at the slices of pizza on display. They're thin and unappealing. A poor attempt to deceive hungry customers. My daughter likes them because they've got sweet corn on them. Where does all this sweet corn come from? Do they put it on everything to get us used to eating animal fodder? There's no real food left in the world. Children are already addicted to sweet corn. Like the stupid women who think it will cure their cellulite, thus removing the only obstacle to the richest and most handsome men in the world falling in love with them.

"A slice of pizza with sweet corn," my daughter tugs my arm.

"And another slice with sweet corn," I repeat as I hand over the money.

I feel weak and dissatisfied that I can't even influence my own daughter. I can't teach her what I think is good. She's seven years old and she already knows more than I do. She's prepared to argue with me. I don't have the strength to argue back. Anyway, it would be ridiculous, a grown man and a little child bickering on the street. I don't want her to eat McDonald's or sweet corn. I want her to have an aesthetic attitude toward food.

I want her to be more interested in the past and in real things (things that I think are real). I truly believe that today's kids take so little interest in the past that it's ceased to exist.

I would like to have some power over this little person—a good and noble power so that I could teach her good things. But I don't.

What good things could I teach her anyway? If she was a boy, I could teach her how to shave when she grew up.

She takes her pizza and starts eating it. She eats and swallows it like it's something inedible. She doesn't seem to be enjoying it. I'm a greedy person. I don't think that the current generation has any idea of the meaning of gluttony. They'll eat seaweed and recycled rubbish, just so they don't have to experience that annoying thing called . . . What was it called? Oh yes, hunger.

When she's eaten as much as her little stomach can hold, and I've eaten the crust and the hard black bits of burnt dough (because I'm a kind person prepared to make sacrifices), we leave, wiping our mouths with paper napkins.

She leads the way while I'm thinking. I'm thinking about food. Food is a pleasure that, in times of insufficiency, is even more shameful than sex. Yes, yes! Don't eat butter, it's full of cholesterol, just like meat. It's bread that kills us. Alcohol makes us fat and stupid, and then it kills us as well. Wine—the blood of Christ—kills us. Whatever!

"Do you like Shakira?" my daughter asks.

"Yes, quite a bit."

"So do I, but . . . not that much."

"Why?"

"Because I like Pink . . ."

"Well, I like her a lot, too."

I'm thinking about the Beatles. I used to really like them. I still do. Like every stupid old man. Why do I like them? Probably because my parents didn't like them. That's so annoying. Why shouldn't I like them? They're brilliant and talented, right? No. I like them simply because my parents didn't like them, they didn't like any kind of music. They liked the songs of Lili Ivanova. They liked gossiping about her and discussing details of her private life, which was probably as absurd as their own.

A beggar crosses our path. He's about as tall as I am. But a little fatter. He looks about sixty. He's wearing an old tram conductor's uniform which has been altered so that he doesn't look like a beggar.

With a bag over his shoulder, so fake-looking it makes me angry. It's as if he wants people to think he's not a beggar, and that the bag's full of sliced bread he's going to feed to hungry children.

"Excuse me, Sir. I'm not a beggar. I just don't have the money to get home. I'm from Pleven. Cross my heart! I wouldn't ask anybody, but you look like a good man. I need the money for the train. I'm not a beggar and I wouldn't ask you if I didn't need the money for the train. Would you give me three levs, so I can get home? God give you strength! I can't stand beggars myself. I just want money for the train, so I can get home. I've got my family waiting for me in Pleven. My grandchildren. May God give your child strength. Give me three levs."

I want to show my daughter what charity means.

I think to myself: He's revolting and looks like a con artist, but she's little and ignorant, and she'll understand that good people don't care who they give charity to. She'll learn how important sympathy and kindness are.

The beggar has a gold tooth, which infuriates me. And I say to myself: Calm down and don't judge people by their gold teeth. I want her to learn how to give and do good.

So I get four levs out of my pocket—one two-lev bill and two one-lev coins. I count out three levs and offer them to him. He snatches them out of my hand and deftly manages to take the other lev as well.

"I just want to get something to eat, I haven't eaten all day."

Even better, I think to myself. My daughter looks at me with a frightened expression.

"Why are you giving him money? He's a gypsy."

"So what? What if he is a gypsy? He's a human being, isn't he, and he needs something, and didn't you hear he hasn't got enough money to get home, and he hasn't eaten all day. It doesn't matter who you give to, what's important is that when you give, it makes you a better person."

Then I spend another five minutes telling her things I don't really believe in, but I would like her to believe in.

But my head is spinning and my heart is thumping with the anger of someone who's been deceived.

I stand on the corner of the street and watch what the beggar is doing with my four levs. My daughter is anxious and tugs my arm. She wants to go. I yank her arm, in turn, and she realizes that I'm dead serious and things aren't as balmy as they were a moment ago.

The beggar walks up and down for a couple of minutes. I know full well that he's looking for another sap, another kind loser to fall for his tricks. But I'm not a kind loser. I just wanted to show my little daughter the nobility of being generous. I wanted to show her that it's good to give, and that when the right hand gives, the left shouldn't know about it. I want her to be generous and kind, and not bitter like everyone else.

I feel furious for doing such a stupid thing.

My daughter looks at me in confusion. She doesn't understand what I'm doing, or what I'm thinking.

The beggar sees me. He looks nervous and goes to a stand for alcohol and nuts. He clumsily pretends that he's buying something. Cashew nuts and bourbon probably.

"The idiot," I think to myself. "Couldn't he have at least gone into the bakery to pretend to buy something? For my sake?"

He sees me again and nods at me. I'm about twenty yards from him, and he pretends to buy something. He's probably expecting me to stop watching. But I carry on.

He pretends to leave.

I tug at my daughter's arm. I pull her toward the entrance of a house, where she asks me in total confusion:

"Are we following him?"

"Yes. He lied to us. He doesn't need any money for a train. You'll see. He's going to ask other people."

"Well, let's go then."

"No, we can't let people lie to us. I'm not going to let him lie to other people."

"Well why did you give him the money in the first place?"

"Because I believed him . . . It's important to give to people who ask, without always thinking they're lying to you."

"Let's go."

"No. If he's a liar, then he's giving back my money!"

I continue to observe the beggar. He realizes that he's free to carry on. He stops a boy and a girl. I can't hear him, but his gestures suggest that he's repeating the same things he said to me.

I feel a thumping in my temples. The sort of anger that sometimes leads to a stroke or murder. I can't explain why. Yes I can. I can give an immediate explanation. I was going to use those four levs to buy some poster paints for my daughter. I wanted her to paint my portrait, just as I am—with a beard and my daughter's love. Now I just feel deceived. But am I a good person? Am I really interested in where the money I gave him is going? Or am I just paranoid and worried about the piece of mouldy bread he's just given to a stray dog?

The blood is thumping in my ears, and the anger and malice is starting to make me feel ill. I squeeze my daughter's hand, and she looks at me with a worried expression.

"It's better to be lied to than to lie to someone else. Do you understand that?" I say in a quiet, hoarse voice.

"Why would people lie to me?"

"That's what people do."

The beggar stops a boy with a backpack. He's one of those distracted sorts of people who live somewhere in the back streets of the Internet. That's when I show myself. I've got a folding knife in my pocket. It's very slender and quite long. It's for stabbing, not for slashing. There must be something wrong with me. I pull my daughter's arm and go up to the beggar. I stand in front of him and at that moment he takes three levs from the boy who lives in the Internet. I press the open knife against his stomach. He makes a stupid, cunning, frightened, and disgusting face.

"Give me my money back!"

"Why? I asked you for some change for the train."

"You're lying." I say harshly and my daughter tugs at my arm. She's very frightened now.

"I wasn't lying. Cross my heart!"

There's a look of arrogance on his face which stops me in my tracks. He looks at me. He can see how worthless I am. He's just pretending to be frightened. He knows all about people like me. If you're the sort of person to give money, you're not the sort of person to kill. With every second that passes, his face becomes harsher and his eyes are no longer filled with that petty cunning, but with cruel and savage disdain. He pushes my hand away.

"And I'm not alone. We're from Pleven. My son's here as well and I have to buy a ticket for him too. And I thought you were a good person."

"Well, if your son's here as well . . ." I don't know what I'm saying. My hand wants to go back to his stomach, to kill him and administer justice. But my mouth just mumbles, "So, your son's here as well? Is that why you're asking everyone for money? Well?"

My voice trembles.

"Get out of my sight! Beat it!"

Angrily and quickly, the beggar turns around and runs down the street. My daughter pulls her hand out of mine and wipes it. We stand there for two minutes. I fold the knife hanging absurdly in my hand.

"Your hand's sweaty," my daughter says.

"Well. I was angry. That old man lied to us."

"Don't worry. I've saved up fifty levs and I'll give you four."

"That's not the point."

I watch the beggar in the distance and I feel so bad, so angry, as if I've just eaten his whole disgusting bag and it's suffocating me. I try to reconcile myself to the situation, but I can't find it in me. My daughter looks at me. Yes! I want to be all-forgiving. I want to be as strong as the ocean tide and as good as a mother with her child. But I can't. My heart is still pounding angrily and my face is covered in perspiration.

"He lied to us. And I . . ."

"What?" my daughter asks.

"I didn't do anything."

"What could you have done?"

"I don't know . . ."

I look at her and see that her mind has wandered back into that distracted, but wonderful, childish Nirvana. She looks at everything as if it's nothing.

I think about what happened for five minutes or so, then my mind wanders off somewhere. We continue to walk along the street, each in our own invisible world.

One of Two Paths

I WAS WALKING along a steep path on the narrow summit of the mountain with bottomless chasms on either side. After about an hour, I reached the top of the mountain and then descended into a small valley overgrown with damp foliage. I could see a cave at the end of the valley between the trees. When I reached the entrance to the cave, I saw who I was looking for. He was sitting a little to one side of it. He was the Wisest Living Man who is said to Know Almost Everything.

He noticed me first. He got up and politely greeted me, offering me a seat on a stone close to the one he was sitting on. The Wisest Man had a very vague appearance—he could be said to be old but not too old, his face was ordinary and kind, his clothes: gray trousers and a greenish short-sleeved shirt.

Was I disappointed? As we sat there, he told me about himself and his extraordinary life, in such a way that his outward appearance seemed to disappear. I had actually come here to ask him something about myself, but he would not stop talking. I listened to the accounts of his hard life, his fight for survival, of pointless and indulgent pleasures, disappointments and delight.

When I realized that his story was complete, I decided to ask him the question I had come here to ask. But he interrupted me with a wave of his hand: "Friend! I know what you want to ask me. I have told you of my life, and perhaps the lives of many other people. But the whole time I was secretly observing the expression on your face and the movements of your body. Thus I know what you want me to say to you. This is what I shall say to you. If you are born without good fortune and are incapable of attaining the least of joy and happiness in the years allotted to you, and believe me there are many people like this, you have two paths: one is to become a good person who loves life and people without reason, the other—to become a desperate and evil monster who hates the whole world. However, I should warn you! Precious few of the people born like you ever take the first path. And now leave me."

I left. I climbed up to the summit and followed the narrow path, on either side of which there yawned bottomless chasms. As I walked I thought about the wise man's words. His words were quite dark. They were a precise answer to my question, but I didn't like them. I could not see any possibility for happiness and joy in my life, but I didn't want to become an angry and malicious person. Absolutely not. As I thought, without realizing, I had slowed down. Finally I stopped and turned around. I thought for a little while more. I was confused. Then I took a deep breath, exhaled noisily and went back. I found my way back to the little valley, descended to the cave and stood in front of the wise man. He was making some soup on a little gas stove.

"What is it, my friend?" he asked as he stood up.

"It's not easy for me to ask you this, but could I stay here with you for a little while?"

"Why?"

"There are a lot of things I want to talk about, as long as you don't mind."

"Well, I get quite bored here, and you could help me carry water and do some shopping for me in the village. No, I don't mind you staying."

"Oh! Really? So I can stay? Thank you. Thank you so much! There are so many things I want to ask you."

"I am sure there are." The wise man bent over the pot and stirred the soup.

"You know . . . I'm really happy you're letting me stay with you."

He stood up, looked at me and smiled contentedly.

"So you're happy . . ."

"Yes, I'm happy."

"So you're experiencing joy?"

"Yes, the joy of soon discovering many things about myself."

"And do you realize that you're experiencing joy?"

I realized that I was happy and understood the strange and ridiculous way in which it had happened. I, a joyless person born without luck or any reason for joy, was happy.

"Well, you got me there!" I said to him, filled with some strange emotion that drove me to the verge of tears.

"Yes . . . I got you!" he said with an air of self-satisfaction. That's why they call me the Wisest . . . I don't know exactly what they said about me. I'm really good at these sorts of things! So you're happy, then?" And he patted me on the shoulder.

"Yes!"

"You can sit here with me and we can enjoy everything together, whatever it might be?"

"Yes, I'll be very happy to sit here with you."

"And just like that, for the fun of it, we'll do some good turns for people?"

"Yes, that's exactly what I want."

"All right then." He patted me on the shoulder. "Have you got any cigarettes?"

"Yes."

"Let's have a cigarette while the soup's on the boil. Then we'll have something to eat, and have a nap in the sun. In the evening you can go into the village to get some beer and do some shopping."

"Yes, now I know why you're the Wisest Man in the World."

"That's right. Give me a light. Thanks!" The wise man lit a cigarette and sat down.

"That's better!" I sat down on the stone as well.

"Yes . . . I'm the Wisest Man in the World," he muttered. "Years ago I was just like you, I mean just like you."

"Really?"

"Yes, I came here to talk to a man . . . It doesn't matter." We smoked our cigarettes and I poured the soup into two bowls and we slurped our soup and wiped away the last drops with bread crust.

"I'm really happy to be here," I said and sighed.

"You're happy now, this evening when we've had our beer, and roast our sausages in the embers and sing, you'll even feel joyful."

"Do you really mean that?" I asked excitedly.

"Yes . . ." The wise man drawled with an air of self-satisfaction. "Now go and wash the dishes."

Problems with the Cleaner

IT IS ELEVEN o'clock in the evening. Outside, the stifling heat of August lies as heavy as an old carpet. Inside, in the little bedroom, the heat is even more stifling. The darkness is as heavy, bitter, and sticky as tarmac. Only the light from the streetlamps on the boulevard falls obliquely through the window to illuminate the small, folded mountain ranges of the white sheets. An old man and woman lie under the sheets. They are lying on their backs, straight as a dye without any bends to ease their bodies. They are lying as if in a coma, their hands placed equally and neatly upon the sheets. For years they have been accustomed to lying motionless in their shared bed in these unnaturally frozen poses in the dark. They do not raise their knees, they do not turn over onto their stomachs or sides, nor do they kick the sheets with their feet. They are accustomed to lying like mummies, since this is best. Turning upsets the sleep.

They are not sleeping. Their open eyes glint in the darkness. They are speaking in muffled voices. They both speak with a lisp since they have removed their false teeth, and now, in the dark, only a handful of loose teeth stick out of their mouths. The old man's voice is low and rumbling, the old woman's tense and whispering. Their voices contain a note of dissatisfaction. The old man's tone is more redolent of astonishment at an act of injustice, while the old woman's voice contains more anger and malice. They are not quarrelling or arguing. The many decades of life together have taught them to be companions in their dissatisfaction. They

26

are capable of pouring out their entire anger and bitterness not at each other, but at someone else, a third person.

If we were to listen to them, we would hear that they are talking about the same old problem that has caused them grief for some time. They talked about it at lunchtime, they talked about it at breakfast time, and they talked about it last night in their stifling bedroom. They've been talking about it for nearly three months.

"She has no right. It's absolutely revolting. I just can't imagine, I have absolutely no idea. She hasn't paid for three whole years . . . she uses the elevator as well . . . and uses the lights on the stairs," the old lady whispers angrily.

"More than anybody else does. First of all, she goes out every day here and there. Secondly, actually if you think about it, those people who live on the eighth floor use it most of all," the old man rumbles angrily.

"No. It's quite straightforward. It's a lack of elementary manners. Haven't they got any conscience? Why don't they pay the cleaner on time?" the old woman whispered in an even crosser voice.

"I went to talk to her and she was very rude. She just poked her head around the door and asked what I wanted."

"Don't get worked up. They're not worth bothering about. The worst thing is that we're left with all the responsibility," the old man's voice rumbles on.

"If Mitko on the eighth floor isn't happy, why doesn't he go round collecting the money himself?" the old woman whispers after a short pause. Her voice contains a certain note of merciless condemnation and unresolved anger with life.

"And what about him! Him, indeed. He always says he's too busy. Busy my foot! A young man like him, twice the size of me. Spends all day playing cards with a can of beer in his hand. All day long. Cigarettes and beer in his hands. That's all I see him doing!" The old man's voice contains a strange note of something akin to pain.

"If it wasn't for us looking after it, who would? So it's the treasurer and cleaner who have to look after the elevator, is that it? Has anybody ever raised money to help pay for repairs?" the old woman crossly asks an unnecessary question.

"And whose job is it to change the light bulb in the elevator? Because I've changed it a dozen times already. Has anybody ever paid a single lev?" the old man quietly rumbles with a hint of bitter frustration. They say nothing for a couple of minutes and they lie in silence in the bitter darkness.

"No, no! I don't want their money!" The old woman breaks the silence. "That's no way to treat us. It's inhuman. They just look at us like . . . it wasn't like that before. Not since . . ." The old woman's voice seems to crack and tremble.

"The cleaner came five times today . . . she comes and rings the doorbell. I open the door and she just walks in," the old woman continues after a slight pause, with the same angry whisper. She clearly wants to move away from the painful subject.

"Yes, you told me . . . So why do you open the door to her?" the old man asks, but his voice is now flat and sad, like someone who doesn't feel well.

"Because she's always asking for something. But she doesn't do anything. She wanted to say that Kalchev on the third floor wasn't happy with her," the old lady explained in a quiet and distracted voice. The old lady and the old man are no longer thinking about what they're saying, but the years have taught them that when there is something important in life, something that causes pain and injury to their old hearts, they shouldn't talk about it. It is better to talk about other things. They are so used to this method of avoiding reality that they have perfected their skills. This time, however, there is something lacking.

"Kalchev's not that sort of person. He's calm like me, just the same," the old man mutters in a monotone.

"She's driving me crazy, ringing five times every day . . ."

"Forget about her! What do you expect her to do?"

"Ah . . . ," the old lady sighs heavily.

"We're going to have problems with her . . . ," the old man mutters.

"There are so many young girls, and boys . . . all unemployed." The old lady's voice is now clearly trembling, and finally muffled.

"Don't get worked up," the old man sighs. "The cleaner might be annoying, but she does a good job."

"No, I'm telling you, she drives me absolutely crazy, and buys the most expensive cleaning products. I saw her one day at the supermarket buying the most expensive ones. 'What's that?' I said. 'Cleaning products for the lobby,' she said. 'Is that right? From now on, I'll buy the cleaning products myself, because all you do is spend our money.' I don't know what she's thinking! She's out of control . . .'"

"We'll have problems with her. But she does a good job cleaning, leave her alone, don't bother her," the old man says in a heavy, muffled voice.

"What if everyone was like that?"

"Don't bother yourself about her . . . I'll talk to her about the expensive cleaning products."

"Are you asleep?" the old lady asks in a softer voice.

"Yes, I'm going to sleep," the old man mutters quietly.

"Good night."

"Good night."

Neither of them moves. They do not shift their sad, rigid, geriatric poses. They just close their eyes, and their eyes no longer glint in the bitter and stifling darkness.

But they are not asleep. Terrifying and ugly thoughts slowly permeate their minds, crushing their aging breasts. They are suffocated by a powerless desolation. They will not fall asleep for a long time yet, but they will lie silently with closed eyes, since the years have taught them to do so when they are feeling at their worst. A terrifying and merciless ghost will haunt the dark, stifling heat between them. They will eventually fall asleep, and as the years have taught them, they will not dream, because if they do, it will be fatal for their old hearts. They know what they would dream, if they allowed themselves to. They will dream of the ghost that appeared three months ago. Three months ago they threw their son out of their house.

Their son had lived with them for the past few years. Those years were a nightmare. He had got divorced, lost his job and his home. He had started drinking heavily and then taken to drugs. He couldn't get any sort of a job, because he was either on drugs or coming off them, shaking and bent double in pain and spasms. To begin with, they hoped they might be able to help him. They forced him to eat and looked upon him with silent reproach. From time to time they would force him into a corner to have a serious conversation. They didn't know what to say, they just said that what he was doing was bad. He listened to them with a bowed head, then he got up and locked himself in his small room.

Then the arguments began. Whenever they saw him stoned or trembling, the old parents would shout at him. The years had taught them not to spare hard words. They told him he was a worthless animal, that people like him should be tortured and killed. They told him that they had had great hopes for him, but he had crushed them. They told him that he was in their way.

After such conservations, he would disappear for a few days. Then he would come back very drunk and stoned and ask for forgiveness and some money so he could come off the drugs. He was a useless, good-for-nothing drug addict and alcoholic.

Finally, his old parents could no longer bear to see him that way, tossing and turning in his little bed, haggard, ugly, unkempt, half-drunk, silent, depressed, and removed from life. One evening they talked to him for a long time and decided that things could not go on like that. They told him to leave in the morning. That was his only salvation, according to them. He put up no opposition. He left with a small bag over his shoulder.

The old parents felt no remorse. The years had taught them that remorse was pointless and bad for your health. They had suffered so much on his account. So what they had done was completely fair.

A few days later, they began to wonder why he hadn't come back to apologize and ask them for forgiveness, to ask for somewhere to stay and some money for cheap booze. They didn't know that their son, their pain, shame, and sickness, that very evening when they had thrown him out, had tied a belt around his neck and had hanged himself in a park shelter.

When they were informed, they bowed their heads and their

arms fell helplessly to their sides. Their fingers fidgeted and they sobbed silently and desperately. How did it happen? they thought, and their tears fell to the floor.

Then they buried him. He was a bad person whose life had been far too short and pointless. He had deserved his ugly end. There was no point mourning such a person. How could you mourn someone like him? the old parents asked themselves. When they were together, they did not mourn, but when they were alone (which was a rare occasion) each of them suffered. They suffered most of all because he had disappeared and not come back to apologize for what he had done to them. Because he was no longer there to become what they wanted him to become, and if he didn't want to, then because they couldn't tell him to get out of their sight.

Nobody came to his funeral. They buried him themselves. They were too ashamed to inform the few relatives they had and their son's few friends of his death. He had left a legacy of shame and emptiness.

Days and weeks passed. They thought about him with lumps in their throats but did not speak. There were other things to talk about. The many years spent together had taught the old people that they had to live. What you might do and what might happen to you, what you feel and what you suffer—none of that matters. They were convinced that they had to live as long as they could, despite everything. And they continued to live.

Life went on, somehow . . .

If it wasn't for the problems they'd been having with the cleaner for the past three months.

A Stroll through Space with
Slight Deviations in Time

YESTERDAY . . . YESTERDAY I was so sad, so unhappy and frustrated, that I put on my stiff blue jacket and went out. It was pouring down outside, the sort of rain I hadn't seen for a long time. Seven-year-old children have never seen rain like it, but they're not so bothered by it and they can't say: "It hasn't rained like this for ten years, not since July 1995." For them, heavy rain is something quite normal, that's how it's supposed to rain. Children don't surprise so easily, they possess within themselves a pre-uterine wisdom. I've seen heavy rains and I've waded up to my waist in mud in the wilderness of Western Bulgaria. I've been very unhappy and frustrated before, that's why I can now say, "I haven't been so unhappy since I don't know when."

I went out in the expectation that the rain would soon drench me—wash me and cool me. I hoped the rain would put me into a state of suspended animation, like liquid nitrogen, and then, like an astronaut, I'd spend my sad and lonely flight into desperation in a state of anabiosis. But that didn't happen. I started walking, but I didn't know where I was going. I left behind me the woman who was the closest person I had, with the exception of my parents, my demented almost one-hundred-year-old grandmother, my daughter, my niece, and another annoying friend of theirs, all of whom I had left behind at home with a vague feeling of relief. She was the only person I felt relaxed with (I could lie on the floor in her house, smoke cigarette after cigarette, fill my glass with drink, watch the rain outside and talk complete nonsense), and now she wasn't there. Or wasn't answering her telephone. Dragged along by the muddy torrents gushing through the streets, as well as those in my brain, I walked toward her house. I called her every ten minutes, more or less every third of a mile or so. Each sad, clipped ring of the unanswered call added another one hundred grams of bitterness, but I kept calling.

I haven't mentioned the reason for my unhappiness and frustration, because I expect everyone knows the only possible reason. But just in case there are people who either don't exist or only pretend to exist, people who don't know the reason, I will tell you: I was alone. Devoid of any hope and alone. Or to be more precise, I was alone, and because of that, devoid of any hope. Whatever. I knew, I was sure, that if I was a more hopeful person, if I was loved, by someone somewhere, or if I could remember good things, which would then remind me of good people, then I wouldn't be alone, even if I was buried in a little titanium capsule a mile below the surface of the Antarctic ice. But I was alone. Even when walking among people, leaving behind the other people in my overpopulated apartment block, surrounded by the noise of voices and car horns. I thought to myself, There is no greater loneliness than that of a person who has been cast out. I thought to myself, There is no greater loneliness that that of the leper walking with his bell warning people of his presence in a town which only moments before had been thronging with people. The people hide, doors slam shut, and he picks up the charity left for him in front of locked doors and goes away again, still ringing his bell. I was alone in the same way, and the waves of brown water lapped over my feet. The water rolled down my eyebrows. I walked but was going nowhere, or rather to someplace where I expected to find reassurance.

Anybody who is reading this might wonder: Why was he alone that evening and why was he feeling so abandoned and leprous? I'll tell you very briefly: I am a bad man and a failure, that's why nobody loves me. That's all there is to it.

All that was left for me to do was to walk and wait for the rain to do something useful, besides flooding the streets and annoying the drivers, whose windshield wipers were too slow. As I walked toward that nowhere which should be better than here (for someone walking, that "here" is the place he finds himself after each step), I wondered why I was such a bad person. It immediately occurred to me that I had never done anything good. But I had done quite a lot of bad things. For example, I had never shown any respect to my parents. I had been lazy and for most of my life I had lived off other people. I had stolen and done a lot of other bad things, like borrowing money and not paying it back (and cutting off all contact with the person who'd given me the money). I had always been irresponsible and completely unreliable. Whenever I did anything good, it had always been for some personal motive, to make me feel proud or great, to tickle my own vanity. At the same time I have always been ready to give up in the face of the smallest difficulty, to grumble and complain, blame Life, People, and the Universe. On top of it all, for as long as I can remember, I've always drunk too much. For as long as I can remember I've taken sedatives, which I'm addicted to. No, no, that's not the reason! I walked along and I thought. A lump came into my throat as I thought about all these things, but I knew they weren't the root cause. The rain splashed me like liquid wheatfields with new granules of water. Is it because I've never cared for anybody? I once took care of a pigeon with a broken wing, but I forgot to feed it, and I didn't put its wing in a splint, and it died. I used it to pretend to be eccentric and impress women with my kindness. No, no, no . . . That's not the reason!

I remembered. That must be it! I've never had enough money to have the confidence to apologize for all the dirt I've done. That must be the reason.

I continue walking and I can't stop, the water is rising, in places even above my ankles. Above my ankles, but not above the ankles of people with umbrellas jumping onto higher, dry spots. I walk, dragged along by the yellowing torrents, the brown downpour. In one place I even see it red and bubbling, as if draining out of a bathtub in which some miserable person has slashed his wrists. It's a horrible sight. I look around to see where this blood-red water has come from. I hadn't noticed that I was walking past a tennis court with a red clay surface. In the state I'm in, completely soaked, twice as hopeless as before, aimlessly and stubbornly walking like a broken walking machine—nothing surprises me.

The water rises up to the middle of the wheels of the cars stuck in the flood. It rains incessantly, not as heavily as before, but incessantly, as if a cursed and evil decision had been made to engulf us in water. I continue walking and can't stop, because when a man is desperate and stops, he dies.

No, I've never had enough money to apologize for all the dirt I've done. To myself and others. I know a lot of people who do this quite well. They perform the most horrible acts and don't feel any sense of shame. They have enough money to pay droves of people to say nice things to them. As I wade through the waves of a miniature Aegean Sea forming in a marble gulley in front of a luxury building, I wonder whether I should be jealous of them or pity them. Whatever. I envy them for some things, pity them for others, and am revolted by the rest.

It's true that I've done a lot of rotten things, and if I had enough money (or filthy lucre as the self-satisfied pigs call it) I would buy whole piles of indulgences and shove them in the face of anyone who opened his mouth to disparage me. When they stare at me with a disapproving look in their eyes . . . More than anything, I'd like to poke out their eyes. I've done a lot of rotten things . . .

I once slept with the future wife of one of my best friends. I did it because he'd been away for a long time; she was lonely and frightened and ready for any kind of intimacy. Another time I stole money from my daughter's piggy bank, because I had a terrible hangover and I needed to drink something. A third time—a third time—at least five women have had to have abortions because of my carelessness, one of them twice. I always abandoned them afterward. In the same way, I abandoned my wife, and now this woman who wasn't answering her telephone. Then I got back together with her, then I abandoned her again, then did the same thing all over.

There's something else, which, in this rain, seems horrible: I like to make friends with drunken vagrants (vagrants are usually drunks, but they're not the only ones). I enjoy taking them to my parents' home to get a good night's sleep. My mother is revolted by the suppurating ulcers on their unwashed feet and throws them out. She's right. I've been living with her since my wife threw me out of the house, and so I have no right to drag contagious scum (which is what I've turned into as well, as my mother likes to say) back to my mother's well-washed, bleached-tile apartment, which looks more like an operating theater. Her home, her castle, her bastion, fortress, and so on . . . built out of the heaviest granite and bronze, with towers of the purest vanadium, is a fourth-floor apartment. When she threw the last vagrant out of her apartment, I felt awful, really guilty for him, her, and before God. I've had a good education, I guess. I look pretty good, I guess, when I'm not drunk. I can talk very politely, but instead of concentrating on my career (I used to be quite a doctor, once upon a time), keeping my hair cut and my nails clean, I fill my mother's home with drifters and drunks (that's what I feel ashamed of before my mother. And before God and the vagrants). My shame is quite clear. Oh God! Why am I so weak and powerless that I can't help another person in need? Don't I know what's good and what's evil? If I can remember what's good, then why don't I defend it, why don't I fight for truth like a lion with two hearts and six bypasses?

I need lots of money to stop feeling desperate. And then people wouldn't abandon me, people would love me and kiss my rosy cheeks whenever they could. I wouldn't be alone. Now all on my own I have to cross an intersection which is so big and so busy that the cars are jammed together. Some of the drivers have gotten out of their cars and are wading through the water. This is not a matter of courage. I've been distracted by my desperation and haven't noticed that the water is up to the sills of the cars. But the smaller cars are now filling with water and their opening doors are making huge ripples. The street is flooded.

I make my way between the cars at the crossroads and notice small groups of policemen trying to bring some order to the chaos, but they look ridiculous in their long black raincoats. If they were to stand on one leg and hold their arms out, they would make splendid scarecrows.

Yes, the rain has inundated the world, but only my legs, back, and head are wet. My heart is dry and sad. Take my friend, K.T.! A couple of days ago he slept with a girl for about ten minutes—a very young girl. And then he chucked her out and ran back to his own wife (Own? Of course, she's his own—he owns her because he bought her with all the money he earns). She says nothing and the anger just builds up, what else can anger do apart from build up? So K. T. has enough money to redeem his Conscience in court. When he chucked out the young girl, he gave her a whole wad of money and she wasn't angry with him. She kissed him on the nose and skipped off like a swallow in October.

But that's not my way. Everyone finds a different, interesting reason to insult and despise me. For example, I don't know if I should tell you this . . . But I am an exhibitionist after all, and I love stripping down in public and revealing the pudenda of my heart and soul. So, once my father tried to suffocate me (the poor old man) and yelled at me until he nearly lost consciousness, saying that I was a "filthy pig" for sitting around with vagrants and drunks, drinking beer. My father, the bitter old man, wouldn't have tried to suffocate or yell at someone with a good job and decent salary of ten thousand levs, or dollars or escudos, or something. And if he did have a decent salary and clean fingernails, it wouldn't matter if he drank a gallon of industrial spirit every day. My father would look on with an expression of quiet hatred and say: "How are things, are you all right? How's your wife?" He might even offer to shake hands, in a gesture of charity and forgiveness. And the man with his ten thousand levs or whatever would stink of whatever industrial alcohol he's been drinking—heating oil, perhydrol, ribonucleic acid. And there would be no mention of "filthy pig" and no suffocation. What a thing money is!

The water reaches up to my knees. Small whirlpools are forming in the water. I wade through them. People are worried and frightened that this might be the beginning of the Great Flood and they'll have to build Noah's Arks, but they'll have to do it in the evenings because they work during the day. The men would miss the games at six o'clock, and the women would miss their soaps at half past six, and life would become wretched. I continue walking, calmer and more confidently desperate. I'm almost drowning and I don't care in the least. I'm not afraid, because I have no intention of building arks, and anyway, I don't go to work during the day. People are worried about the Flood, because it will drench them, it will flood their houses, their parquet flooring will swell up and there will be much wailing and gnashing of teeth, and they might even catch cold.

I walk past a low spot resembling an urban marsh, a puddle as big as Lake Erie. An elderly lady is up to her waist in water. She's waving her tired arms, but nobody's looking at her, because everyone is rushing about their own business, to their own sweet life, to their own wretched death. I'm annoyed that the woman might drown, then the police will have to come, hang around for a bit, prod around with poles in the water and silt. They'll smoke cigarettes and talk about football, they'll find her pale, swollen body and they'll load it into an ambulance, so that her relatives can mourn her, light candles, and other rubbish like that. It really gets under my skin.

I head toward the woman. The silt is very heavy and pulls me down. The ground wants to swallow me up, but I don't care, because I'm a filthy, repulsive man, and the earth will regurgitate me as soon as it tastes me. I get to the woman, she's firmly stuck in the mud and her eyes are filled with fear. I smile insanely at her, like a shopkeeper handing her a box of laundry detergent from the top shelf. I don't know how to smile at her any other way. What sort of smile can you give when you're up to your neck in water? You'd smile just like I did, even though it frightened her a bit.

"Let's have a look at you, you really are stuck in the mud, grab hold of me and I'll pull you out."

"Oh my God! My son! Save me, save me! I don't want to die here. I've got a boy like you."

"What, a bastard like me?" I mutter, she sobs in fright and wails:

"Oh, I'm going to die!"

"One day for sure, but not now. Stop squirming, you're just sinking more! Give me your hand. Come on!"

"Help me, my son, let me get hold of you."

"That's what I just said," I replied angrily. "Isn't that what I've been telling you? Grab hold of me and I'll pull you out."

"Oh God! Help me. I'm scared we'll drown."

"Didn't I say something to you?" I pull her out by the arms. "There's nothing we can do about it. There's no two ways about it . . . Try not to move your feet, just swim with your arms, the mud's dragging you down."

"Oh God!"

"God's not going to help! Is now the time to think about God? Come on, don't give up," I shout angrily and pull. We're almost out. We're both covered in sticky mud and water tainted with rotting rats and rainbow-colored slicks of motor oil.

We wade out of the deep water and the old lady is sobbing. She tries to hug me, and kiss me, but I'm already moving on, splashing through puddles up to my knees. The rain slowly begins to ease off and then stops. The water starts draining away into the sewers, the sun even comes out—a strange, droll sort of evening sun—just before it hides behind the mountain peak of Vitosha to go on to somewhere else.

I continue splashing through the puddles, heading someplace where I hope I might find solace.

Eighty Thousand Leagues under
the Ladies' Market

A MAGAZINE CALLED *Egoist* commissioned me to write a travel article. The editor-in-chief wanted it to be something like a lifestyle piece. As far I knew the magazine, that meant a piece aimed at young, self-satisfied nouveau riche who dreamed of being isolated from the world and its shameful pain while wearing three-hundred-dollar flip-flops. I accepted the commission and asked myself what "lifestyle" meant. Perhaps it meant describing the places of interest that I'd walk right past, where the same self-satisfied girls and boys could buy clothes to shield their helpless nakedness from real life?

So I went to the Ladies' Market. No later than half past ten in the morning. Why did I choose that particular place on an empty October morning? Is it because I have a special attitude toward ladies, or because the market's old name was Georgi Kirkov and that reminds me of the surrealist Giorgio de Chirico? I couldn't say.

I decided against taking the busy route via Maria Louisa and Lion's Bridge. There's something offensive and dirty about that route, reminiscent of a congealed drop of gypsy sperm. I walked along the dusty street toward the freight station, a place of dreams for everyone addicted to sniffing wallpaper glue. It's a dusty place. I crossed Levski Boulevard and began my journey along Kiril and Methodius Street.

Little journeys like this are magical. Whoever's gone to get beer at the closest neighborhood shop will never want to go anywhere else. See Block Eighteen in Banishora and die. Little journeys are like looking into jewels and seeing all the details and facets. Every yellowing leaf, every blade of grass, every lichen. The lichen on the faces of the sad people of the city, desiccated by their mediocre lives.

I walk through the soft October morning down the long narrow street. The old, yellowing houses, are not yet as bloated or moldy as those on the old boulevards. There are empty windows here and there. But there are signs of stubborn life almost everywhere. So there is life here on our planet Earth after all, I think to myself. Everywhere I look, I see small shops where life slowly and unerringly flickers. There are little shops for repairing buttons, rewinding electric motors, and repairing old coffee pots. The mysterious ways of old coffee pots.

A boy in a black suit and red shirt buttoned to the top without a tie is standing in front of the door of a violin repair shop. He looks like a victorious soldier returning from the latest war, which was probably fought against people dressed in yellow shirts, blue suits, and bowties.

I see a thin, decrepit woman, poor and unrecognizable from alcohol. She knocks on the door of a derelict house and calls out a woman's name. In her hand as thin as a sparrow's leg, she's holding half a slice of bread not spread but spattered with margarine. I first thought it was butter, but then I sadly realized that these people don't have butter. She was calling out a woman's name and I realized that she was taking this half a slice of bread to a woman who was even poorer and more decrepit than she was. Lifestyle. Style of our life.

I see a man and a woman playing backgammon in a little shop selling chips and wafers, not full but not empty. Isn't it a bit early for backgammon?

I reach the Ladies' Market.

Where there's decay, there's life. In the Ladies' Market decay and life are so interwoven that they're indistinguishable. Very intense as well. I don't just want to see what's happening in the Ladies' Market, I want to see things that other people don't. And I want to make some wise conclusions as well, if I can.

If you leap from stall to stall, if you ask questions, stick your nose in and annoy people, you won't find anything out. You have to sit quietly, in a state of sad serenity, and observe. Grasshoppers are fools, spiders are wise. If you sit aimlessly for a few hours in an aimless place, you begin to discover strange things. For example, the waitress in an aimless restaurant is pointlessly jealous of the owner's wife.

I sit down close to the middle of the market in a small cafe where you can eat revolting food, drink toxic drinks, and get smashed in the teeth by the locals if you're a smart-ass. And my observations begin.

Meat, so much meat. I just want to remind you that what you're reading at the moment is a lifestyle article. Fashion. Meat ads, gypsies, people selling earbuds, buckets of butter, and lighter flints. And a madman walking through the market. I'll tell you about him later.

So much meat. Behind glass, in front of glass, in dreary corners of decaying shops, hanging on hooks like a public display of dissected horses. The meat shops are predominantly Arab. The Bulgarian shops aren't interesting. The Arabs clearly possess a special sort of ancient genius for inventing glazed outdoor mortuaries. Even the most passionate carnivore would quiver with disgust at the sight of the Arab shops selling veal throats and lamb appendices. Some people say the Lebanese and other Arabs are more civilized than the Bulgarians. When I see the bluish flesh of calves lying on the greasy, marble countertops, I realize that this is not the case. In one of the shops, a dark-skinned man is cutting a bright-red cut of meat. Between two slices of his knife, he eats a cheese pie. A fat woman enters the shop and sits down on a chair in front of the counter. In a very familiar way. "How much is the tripe?" the old lady asks. "One fifty," the Arab says. "Is it cleaned?" the old lady asks. "No, not cleaned." "One fifty and not cleaned! You must be joking! You should be ashamed!" the old lady says, and a quiet, unattractive, but friendly clash between Christianity and Islam ensues.

Between the bakers and the butchers, I can glimpse the public restrooms made out of aluminum and glass, and two strutting twenty-year-old gypsy toilet attendants standing in front of them. They are aristocrats in spirit; Brahmins among the lowest castes of pickpockets and sellers of cassette players stolen out of parked cars. Then my gaze turns to two women. I watch their backs as they pass by. Nobody could have such long legs, such proud bearing and jet black hair. Within a radius of about two, two and a half yards around them, the spirit of New Orleans seems to waft. Gypsy prostitutes, I think to myself, and I follow them.

When they get to the public toilets, the gypsy prostitutes (that sounds a bit nasty and priggish) say: "Oh, cutey! How are you darlings?" They're aristocrats, so they speak Bulgarian rather than Roma. The toilet attendants kiss them behind the ears, say something funny, and light cigarettes.

I stand bleakly about eight yards from them and admire them. These are the people who will infuse new blood into the fair-skinned people of Europe, not me. Nope! I sit in another cafe and order a beer.

It's twelve o'clock. In front of me there is an old man who has suffered a couple of strokes in his sad, bowed head; he's selling ear picks. I think to myself, Why doesn't he sell eye picks? These you would use to prop open the eyelids of your enemies, leaving them outside to stare at the sun. What do people need ear picks for? I wonder. Where does this quivering human individual, with hair like the dusty fluff balls from under your bed, get them? I look into his eyes and see everything illustrated there: where, how, and why. Nobody should be exposed to what lies in the dirty, sick eyes of this old man. It's too horrible. But I have to be accurate in my descriptions. Let me remind you, this is all just lifestyle.

I go up to the old man and buy enough ear picks for the next two years, if I had twenty-seven ears. The old man can't talk very well, because the speech center in his brain has been damaged. He mumbles something. I realize how disgusting people are who are more interested in two-hundred-dollar flip-flops than they are in somebody like him.

Behind me, somebody is selling shelled walnuts heaped up in piles. The residents of the Ladies' Market are resourceful people, I say to myself. They go to the trouble of shelling walnuts so they

can sell them at a moderately higher price. I go to a nearby stall
and buy a Jewish sandwich.

Jewish sandwiches are more interesting than banal Arab doner
kebabs. They probably contain at least four different versions of
minced soy. I once ate something Arabic called a *kube*. It was a
ball of extremely fatty, heavy mutton, at least I think it was mutton, mixed with whole walnuts. Ever since then I've preferred the
Jews to the Arabs. I find their lifestyle more acceptable. That's
how you turn into a racist, for God's sake.

I see a fat man walking between the stalls, eating a wafer. He's
looking at the food on sale. He's not particularly interested in
the beetroot and prunes. He's looking at the smoked meats, fatty
bacon, sausages, chicken fillets, endless coils of salami, which
with their evil, sickly appearance would scare off any normal,
healthy European. I follow the fat man and see him buy a loaf of
bread and then a portion of smoked breasts, as fatty as his and
abnormally yellow. This is the lunch of either a local stallholder
or a thief. He's so fat I fear for him. Bulgarians in general are fat
and I fear for them all. (With the exception of the wives of the
former crime bosses—now bankers—who go to gyms to keep
thin, to please their fat pigs of husbands who reek of stupid
death, and to get presents like little jeeps or a fist in the teeth
for International Women's Day, New Year's, and their birthdays.)
It's just lifestyle.

I continue my walk around the Ladies' Market. I leave the fat,
greasy man with his greasy food in his hands to get even fatter
and die early of a heart attack. I walk toward a dead-end street
with a sign that reads: "Nightingale—Culture Committee." I've
never seen such a wretched, old, and out-of-place sign, and I've
seen plenty of signs in my life. It stands in a place where nobody
can see it, above the entrance to some nondescript cooperative
block. I enter. Inside a completely drunk man is yelling: "I'm
sorry! I'm sorry to the whole of the Ladies' Market. I'm sorry!"
Farther inside, in the depths of the cooperative, two men are sitting at a table drinking beer. They clink their two bottles against
a third unopened one, most likely they're remembering a dead
friend. The men are young, but life in the Ladies' Market is short

and brutal. At the far end of the block a middle-aged man is dragging a twelve-year-old gypsy by the hair into a dark, gloomy stairwell. She doesn't resist and skips around him nimbly, because she's got experience. He's probably taking her somewhere to punish her or to have sex with her, I imagine. I feel devastated.

I go out of the crumbling cooperative into the October sun and the noise. From time to time, above the noise, I hear the voices of gypsies trundling barrows loaded with goods: "Watch out!" I think to myself that this is the voice of the prophet telling these mad people: "Watch out! Since Armageddon is at hand, when the kings of the world shall face each other for one last battle and all will become clear." The people indifferently make way for the barrows, curse, and continue buying and selling, because that's why they've come to the Ladies' Market.

A madman walks through the market with his head bowed. The veins on his neck are swollen and he shouts in a calm, but even voice: "Then the Americans will flatten Afghanistan with their bombs and they will go to heaven, and every one of them will have three Kuwaiti bitches, three Kuwaiti bitches who will sit on their dicks. Aha . . . !" I follow the madman, but he walks in a circle around one section of the market shouting the same thing over and over. Still, I like him, because he's an anti-globalist and states his opinion boldly. Bulgarians don't have censorship anymore, and for that reason they don't have any opinions on anything. They're not interested in anything, because nothing's banned anymore and they're not interested in anything. If there is one opinion shared by all the people in the Ladies' Market, then it's that they're not interested in this madman, nor are they interested in anything else apart from half-heartedly and indifferently buying and selling goods. This is the style of their life.

I go to a bleak corner of the market which is being dug up. People try to avoid the mud, rotting fruit, and plastic bags by leaping across narrow planks. They're all wretched, sickly, ugly, and filthy. I start thinking about those crazy middle-aged, boyish politicians, economists and so on, with their necks stuck out and eyes popping, trying to convince the fair-skinned inhabitants of Europe to take in these people and give them a place to live, perhaps in the corner next to the cooking stove. And the fair-skinned, healthy Europeans basted with a layer of fresh butter will laugh, show their white teeth and say: "Oh, no, no! Ha, ha! No!"

I stand in this revolting corner and a little gypsy girl comes up to me and says, "Five levs for a blow job, mister!" And I say, "Five levs? Get out of my sight. You should be ashamed of yourself . . ."

Then I leave the Ladies' Market and go to the Hali closed market. The atmosphere is tranquil, clean, and smells like discrete stupidity. There's nothing decaying here and so there's no life. There aren't any Bulgarians here, I think to myself. This is just a place for people who want to imagine that they live better than dogs, who do everything they can to imagine such a life, so much so that they become depersonalized. They walk in a quiet, educated manner between the tidy stands full of the most diverse garbage made from PVC and polyurethane, and think that they've discovered their own lifestyle. I am overcome by a feeling of sadness among this calm and cheery consumer wilderness, and I go back to the Ladies' Market to follow the madman. And five levs isn't so much money after all.

Fights

HE COMES HOME at two o'clock in the morning and he's very drunk. No, he's not drunk. He's just full to the top with alcohol. A drunk is someone who has imbibed alcohol. He is just alcohol without anything else. He's drunk a huge amount, he's completely saturated with drink, but he doesn't want to drink anymore because he feels guilty.

"Where have you been?" his sleepy wife asks him.

"I've been . . . all over the place . . ." He hasn't got the strength to lie. Not because he's got a conscience, but simply because he's powerless to lie right now.

"Where?"

"Lots of places . . . I'm going to bed."

Until now she's been lying on her side half-asleep, but now she gets up and looks at him.

"So where have you been?"

"Why are you asking me? I went where I wanted to."

"You know I've been waiting for you?"

"I thought you were asleep?"

"I just dozed off a moment ago. So where have you been? You reek of alcohol."

"We've been drinking."

"Of course you have . . . Who've you been with?"

"With my friends."

"Which ones?"

"The doctor and that . . . taxi driver . . . Aren't you asleep?"

"Why didn't you call me?"

"I did, but there wasn't any coverage."

"I'm sure. And so what? You got drunk and now you're dragging your ass back to me, and going to bed in your clothes. Reeking of alcohol."

"I suppose so."

He's unhappy because he feels weak. His legs are giving in because of the alcohol, the feeling of guilt, and the heavy sense of pointlessness.

"That's great. Just incredible. I have to go to work tomorrow and it's three o'clock." Then suddenly in a very loud and angry voice: "Don't you understand that I can't put up with it anymore? You come home at three o'clock as drunk as a pig, and I have to sit here and put up with it. No. No, no!"

"Come off it. That's enough. Are you awake now? I'll open a bottle of wine."

"Why *don't* you just open another bottle. Doesn't look like I'm going to get any more sleep. There's no end to your disgusting behavior. If you want to behave like that, go on, I can't."

"Come on now. That's enough . . ."

A little uncertain on his feet, he opens a bottle of wine and calms down. He pours out two glasses and takes a swig out of the bottle to calm himself a bit more.

They sit together in silence, smoking. The wine they're drinking is warm and tasteless. He stares at the dark, white ceiling with blue reflections of the television pointlessly working in the background.

"And where did you drink?" she asks abruptly, because she's impatient to hear something bad.

"With a couple of friends. I told you, didn't I?"

"Women?"

"Yes," he says, suddenly raising himself on his elbows. He wants to say something vulgar and bold. He wants to be honest but the weakness in his eyes, in his brain and in his heart, stop him from speaking.

"What do you mean by 'yes'?"

He lies down again and relaxes, surrendering and wanting only to cry and sleep. If he could, he would admit to everything in his sleep. He wants to cry and to confess while he sleeps.

"We were with these . . . They were prostitutes. We went to a club, that's where we were."

She's calm, because she realizes that at this moment she has to be calm. She wants to lose her temper, but doesn't want to do it straight away. She has to wait for the malice to accumulate and for the anger to open her mouth.

"And?"

"Nothing, I talked to one of them. I paid her for talking, we talked about things like bringing up children, cooking, that sort of nonsense. I wanted to talk to someone."

"So you can't talk to me?"

"I can."

He wants to go to sleep, but he's worried. He's scared of the anger building up inside her, and he knows that it won't end there.

"And how much did you pay her?"

"Sixty levs . . . that's how much it costs . . ."

He's annoyed by this petty detail, but he's weak. He feels helpless to stand up to the pointlessness he's feeling.

"So, what are we going to live on now?"

"I'll get some more money tomorrow. Don't worry." He tries to offer her his hand in the dark. "I haven't slept with another woman . . . I haven't been unfaithful . . ." He calms down a bit, since he thinks he's said something reassuring which will resolve the situation.

She lies there and looks at the ceiling. She trembles and puts her hand over her eyes. She suddenly starts talking slowly. At first her voice is quiet and low, then gets louder and more frightening. By the end she's yelling at him.

"You came to live with me. You don't give me anything. I can't expect anything from you, and you have the gall to come back home as drunk as a pig. You get into bed with me and then you tell me you've been with a prostitute, and you've given her all your money, and you don't care . . . oh my God!" She bursts into tears. "Why, oh why? What have I done to deserve this?"

He raises himself up again. He feels dizzy, but he's wide awake and his heart is thumping in his throat.

"Hold on . . . what am I to blame for? I was just talking to a woman."

"Talk to whoever you want to. You're all pigs. All of you . . . How I hate you." She sobs inconsolably.

"All right! If that's what you think." He turns over. He's upset but relieved that it's come down to sobs and vague accusations. That doesn't scare him, because he knows that women cry and then fall asleep. "All right, all right! If that's what you think."

Half an hour later and he's falling asleep. He tosses and turns anxiously, but in the end falls into a deep sleep with his chin sticking up, snoring loudly.

She isn't sleeping. She turns over and looks at him in the dark. Her face looks as sour as if she's been eating a lemon. She's experiencing intense hatred and repulsion. She gets out of bed, goes into the other room and gets an old, warped guitar without any strings, which has been sitting there as long as she can remember.

She comes back into the bedroom and stands in front of the bed for a moment. He's asleep with his legs spread out, his arms folded over his chest, resembling somebody who's died from typhus.

She kicks him. "Wake up!"

He just mumbles in his sleep.

She imagines the revolting things he's done. She's upset by the thought that he's paid a woman to talk to him. She's got so many things she wants to tell him, but he's been talking to a woman he doesn't even know. She kicks him again. "Wake up! Do you hear me? I want to talk to you. Wake up!"

He just turns his face to her. His mouth is open and it stinks of alcohol, the woman, and filthy, bad things.

She waves the guitar and hits him. The first hit is along the diagonal line of his nose. He's startled, but so stunned by the blow he doesn't move. His eyes are open and blink sleepily. He doesn't even cry out. The second blow is on his forehead. The third blow hits the pillow and his ear. It splits and something dark like blood pours onto the pillow.

In her fury she takes another five or six blows, but weaker and less accurate.

He's awake now. His face is covered in blood. He says nothing and his eyes blink vaguely in the darkness. He gets up. Without a sound, neither of pain or anger. With his whole body, he throws himself at her and pushes her to the ground. She doesn't say anything either. She just moans tensely. He holds her down with his chest, knees, shoulders and begins striking her face rhythmically, not very hard, but with the full hatred of a man who has felt his life threatened. He hits her for five minutes. Then he gets up, goes to the other room, gets his jacket and some clothes. He leaves silently.

She is lying beaten and quietly whimpering. Her face is covered in blood, tears, and hair, and everything else that comes out of a face after being punched so many times.

When she hears him fiddling with the lock of the door, then opening it and closing it after him, she feels a wave of anger. She laughs out loud. "Ha! He's gone! The animal's gone."

Two minutes later, she's crying and wiping off the blood with a cloth.

She feels scared. What is she going to do all night, alone, beaten, crushed by desperation, contempt, and fear?

She runs outside. She can see him in the dark about a hundred yards away leaning on a streetlamp.

She goes up to him. She takes him by the hand. He looks at her, then carefully raises his hand and touches her cheek. She pulls his arm. He follows her. As they walk, she gently puts her arm around his waist. He sobs loudly and desperately. She squeezes him tighter. They go up into the apartment and go to bed. They are both in pain, but slowly and hesitatingly they embrace. They aren't alone. Now, at least for a second, they are not afraid. Everything that happened still exists, but for a moment it doesn't matter. Their hands tremble and sob more than their eyes. They embrace with all the tenderness of the world. They kiss each other's desperate, sick face. Their hope rests in God, to save them . . . This is real love.

In the morning she makes him breakfast.

The recipe of what she made him for breakfast is the subject of another story.

A Christmas Triptych

CHRISTMAS. DECEMBER 25, 2008. Sofia, Bulgaria.
On Tsarigrad Boulevard, very close to the Ring Road, an old
Opel and even older Volkswagen hit each other side-on causing
a lot of damage. There's nothing particularly strange about that.
Two young families were traveling in the cars. One of them con-
sists of I.B., who owns a shop selling stolen cell phones, and his
wife, S.B., a hairdresser and owner of a beauty parlor in what
used to be a cellar.

The Volkswagen belongs to I.M., a carpenter at a furniture
company, and L.S., a secretary in an advertising agency. They're
not legally married but have been living together for three years.

The men have emerged from the incident with nothing more
than extreme nervous anxiety caused by the idiocy and incompe-
tence of the other driver. The women are in a much worse state.
S.B. has a badly broken nose and a lot of little glass cuts on her
face. L.S. has a broken shinbone in her left leg.

S.B. is sitting in the car, sobbing and sniffing blood. L.S. is in
a state of shock and is blinking in fright. She is lying on the blan-
ket which her husband has laid out for her on the ground. She
doesn't dare look at her leg which is painfully bent. The two men
are standing twenty paces away from each other facing opposite
directions. They have their backs to each other (like at a pistol
duel) and they're speaking on their cell phones to car-mechanic
friends. They're smoking ferociously and explaining the probable
damage to their cars.

The smashed-up cars are holding up traffic, drivers swear at

53

them as they pass by. Women passengers in the passing cars tut and scold.

It's been ten minutes since they called for an ambulance. It's snowing heavily in small, sharp flakes.

A battered Golf stops in front of the crashed cars. Two young men with red faces get out. One of them is short, the other taller. They go up to L.S., who is lying on the ground. They nod politely and ask an astoundingly stupid question: "How are you? How do you feel?" When they notice that the woman is in shock and is moving her lips without speaking, they go over to S.B. "How are you?" they ask, again politely and idiotically nodding their heads. The short one even bows slightly, which looks completely absurd, since S.B.'s wound is so deep the bones of her nose can be seen.

"Well, if you don't want to talk," the two red-faced men say. "We're doctors and it's our duty to help you." For some reason they both smile.

The tall one gets his first-aid bag out of the Golf. They get out bandages to make compresses and fabricate splints. The short one goes over to L.S. He bends down over her and with a strong, sharp tug straightens her broken leg, then he puts it between the splints and wraps it up with the bandages. He takes an ampoule of diazepam out of his pocket, fills a disposable syringe and gives her an injection. "This isn't really the right thing to do," He mumbles as he holds L.S.'s hand. He pats her lightly on the cheek from time to time. A few minutes later, L.S. stops trembling and rolling her eyes. "Your leg's broken," the red-faced man bending down over her says. "But there's nothing to worry about." He smiles and L.S. remembers to cry: "Oh God, my children. Oh my God!" L.S. sobs quietly. "Shut up!" The red-faced man orders her. Despite her anxious state and the pain, L.S. smells the head-turning stench of alcohol on his breath. "The children are fine. Everything's fine. Just lie here and don't move!" the man orders and goes to see what his friend is doing. On his way over he takes a flat metal flask out of his pocket and takes a swig. The tall man has just cleaned the wound. He's gathered the flaps of skin and inserted cotton wads in her nostrils. He takes the flask and has a swig as well. "So you're doctors, are you?" S.B. asks in an angry voice. "Yes, oh yes, we're doctors," the red-faced men laugh and hand each other the flask, "that's why we offer our help to anybody in need. Isn't that so?" They give each other a strange look. "Are those your husbands over there?" The tall man asks pointing at them with the flask. "Yes, they are . . . ," S.B. sniffs. "Well, you tell them from me . . . ," the tall one says wringing his hands in satisfaction. "Tell them from me that they're miserable bastards!"

The men wait for the ambulance to arrive. They speak to the doctor and help load the women in. The drivers of the crashed cars are still preoccupied with explaining the damage to their cars to their car-mechanic friends. The ambulance leaves, the drivers of the crashed cars watch them go without interrupting their conversations.

The strange red-faced doctors go back to their battered old Golf. As he walks past one of the men who is still talking about his wheel rims, the tall doctor hits him in the back so hard that the man falls to his knees. He turns around ready to fight, but his eyes are met by a gaze which makes him feel like bird shit and his stomach churns. "Merry Christmas, bird shit!" the short one greets him. The two red-faced men get into their Golf and disappear into the cold, sharp snow.

The cold, sharp snow stings like needles, especially the nose and cheeks. Nellie the prostitute, whose name isn't Nellie at all, is standing in a doorway near Lions' Bridge. She's chain-smoking and is angry that she's been punished. She was beaten by her pimp last night, because he found out from one of her colleagues (the filthy whore) that she'd been paid double by one of her clients, one hundred levs, but lied that he'd only paid the normal going rate. Now here she is at Christmas, alone in the cold, and what mad idiot is going to look for a prostitute on Christmas? The damn gypsies in the apartment blocks have fitted them with automatic doors and you can't get inside into the warm. Nellie goes over to the bus stop to buy herself a coffee. She's walking through a snow drift when a battered Golf pulls up along the sidewalk. Two men get out of it—one of them short, the other tall. They're both red-faced, and Nellie, who's experienced in these matters, sees that they've been drinking since lunchtime. Nellie really hates drunk clients, because they're oafs and pigs. Not that the others aren't pigs, but drunks can become violent and perverted. Her pimp's like that. He just needs to have a drink and whatever she says to him—she gets a beating. With his fists, and then she has to show off her bruises to clients and colleagues.

The men approach and Nellie is happy. Drunk, sober, they're all clients and at least she'll be warm. That's right!

"How are you, my fine lady?" the short man asks and takes a flat metal flask out of his pocket. He takes a drink and hands it to the other. "Are you looking for a girl?" Nellie examines them with her professional eye. "No, not just a girl, no! We're looking, we're looking for truth and beauty, and what else?" the short one turns to the tall one. "And . . . perfect harmony and the splendor of female companionship, because we don't want to be alone on Christmas," the tall one hiccups. "You're not a couple of madmen, are you?" Nellie asks suspiciously and looks at them. They don't look crazy, they look normal, she thinks to herself. "No, no, we're not madmen, we've just had a bit to drink, in order to abscond for a moment from the deep sadness which is stifling our hearts on this marvelous feast day, for the love the Savior gave us, which has nobody to receive it," the short one accepts the flask and takes a long swig. "Well, if we're going to do something, why don't we go back to your place, or my hotel?" Nellie asks.

"Oh, so you have a hotel?" The tall one slips and almost falls over. "There's a hotel here, just round the corner," Nellie laughs and points, "let's go." The men follow her. Suddenly one of them stops her with his hand. "What?" Nellie pushes his hand away. "Well, we don't want to spend Christmas in a hotel, which isn't yours and is just the one around the corner. Let's go somewhere else, somewhere nice." "Where? I won't go anywhere away from the center." Nellie says suspiciously. "We're not going away from the center, we want to go to the center," the short one makes funny gestures. "Well, all right," Nellie walks on. They follow her, walking deliberately through the snowdrifts left by the snow-plow. They hand each other the flask and talk nonsense.

They get to a little street behind the Central Store. Nellie sees that it's a posh place. She feels awkward because she's wearing home-knitted stockings under her short skirt and even the powder on her face won't hide the bruises from last night. They are standing in front of a very shiny restaurant. They don't look rich, Nellie thinks to herself, is it a whore trap? Nevertheless, they go in, like they're at home, and head over to a table as if they already know which one. They stand next to the table, and the short one pulls out a chair and invites her to sit. No, he's screwing with me, Nellie thinks to herself, they're having a laugh. I bet they haven't got any money. "Have you got any money?" Nellie asks standing suspiciously. "Well, yes, if that really matters. Have a look." The tall one puts his hand in his pocket and takes out such a wad of money that Nellie has only ever seen the like of it in films, and once when she was with an Arab client.

They sit down. The waiter comes over and the short one orders: "Champagne, my dear man, black caviar, cod-liver paste, and ten grouse eggs." "We haven't got anything like that." The waiter looks at them coldly and looks at the men's red faces and the girl's blue face. "Do not give up your wonderful profession just because of such a small omission, my good sir," the tall man says. "Then bring a portion of filet mignon for the young lady, because she looks upset and hungry. Isn't that so?" The tall man looks at her in a rather peculiar way. "And what is most important, Merry Christmas, my dear waiter." He stretches out his hand and pinches the waiter on his shaven cheek. The waiter wants to call for security, but he's stopped in his tracks by the look in the tall man's eyes. His shaven chin begins to tremble, and he feels as if he wants to burst into tears and asks for forgiveness.

Half an hour later Nellie has drunk the whole bottle of champagne and is completely giddy. However, she's enjoying herself and laughing because the two men are talking such nonsense to her. They tell her that they have fallen from the sky. "That's what they look like," Nellie grins. Her filet arrives and she eats like a pig, because she hasn't eaten since yesterday and it's already late afternoon. The two men watch her. They smile and continue only to take swigs out of the flask. They pour the whiskeys they order into the flask; they don't want to drink out of glasses. They don't eat anything. "You're not normal!"

"Young lady, may I ask you where the bruises on your face came from?" the short one asks, hiccupping and covering his mouth with his fist. Nellie suddenly remembers her pimp and quivers. The champagne goes to her feet. "Oh my God! Are you going to pay me, you know, without screwing me?" "Yes, of course, didn't we tell you we were looking for companionship?" The tall man puts a wad of bills into her lap under the table. She waits for a moment and then looks at the money. There must be more than three hundred levs! "So, where did you say you got the bruises on your face?" the tall man asks. Nellie laughs with joy and the champagne once again rises to her head. "It was that pig, my pimp. He hit me last night. I really hate drunk men." "So you hate us?" The short man looks at her in astonishment.

"Oh no! You're really brilliant guys! You're completely weird!" Nellie laughs and pats him on the shoulder so hard that the short man almost falls off his chair. "So what are we going to do now?" Nellie asks and pours herself champagne from the second bottle, which has mysteriously appeared.

"Well, that's a marvelous question," the short one says. "First we're going to drink until we've had enough, then you're going to go home to your boyfriend, and you're going to tell him that he's a miserable bastard, and that if he ever lays his hands on you again, he'll have some very dangerous people to contend with. And as for us, we'll just go about our business. Here's another little present for you," the short one says and puts a small perfume bottle on the table in front of her. "What's that?" Nellie asks, becoming suspicious again. "It's not drugs is it?" "No, kind lady," the short one smiles very curiously. "This is medicine. You just put one drop into your . . . bastard's . . . drink, and he'll become as obedient and sweet as a little lamb. But it will make him puke a lot." "Do you want me to poison him?" Nellie replies joyfully. "Nonsense, nobody's going to die. He'll just stop drinking. If he doesn't want to puke his guts up . . ." "You're completely out of your minds," Nellie laughs and spills champagne on her blouse. "Merry Christmas, kind lady," the short one says, raising the metal flask. "You're completely insane!" Nellie raises her glass. "Merry Christmas." The tall one takes the metal flask and drinks.

It is drawing toward evening and getting colder. On Chavdar Bridge, leaning against the railings, stands M., a forty-year-old dental technician who has just split up once and for all with his wife, B. They've split up six or seven times over the past year, but this time looks like it's going to be final. Because it's Christmas and M. has had enough of it all. He doesn't really understand why his wife has grown to hate him so much that she might as well want him dead. He's got the feeling she wants to kill him. Not just to kill him, but to destroy him, to dissolve him in sulphuric acid, or sodium hydroxide. It's true that M. is not perfect. But who is perfect, for God's sake? M. thinks and a lump comes into his throat. Nobody! What do I do that other men don't? I don't earn a lot. Yes! That's what it is! But everything else . . . She thinks I'm an idiot and a failure. Perhaps. But on the other hand, there are lots of losers and idiots who get on well with their wives. Not everyone can be clever and successful. Isn't that so? That's not the point. She just hates me with all her soul, and thinks that had her life turned out in any other way, it would have been better than this. And that I'm the reason for all the bad things that have happened in her life . . . Yes! But on the other hand?

I'm not a womanizer. I'm not a drunk. It's true that I have a drink with my friends in the evenings in the bar in our block of apartments, but I might as well be at home. And she comes and shames me in front of everyone: "It's time you came home! You're as drunk as a pig, come on, you're tripping over your feet!" she shouts and embarrasses me in front of the neighbors. Then, when we get home she looks at me with such spite, slams all the doors and makes faces. My daughter's on her side. They sit there looking at me as if I was a criminal. I go into my little room, like I'm a lodger. But I know they're sitting in the living room saying bad things about me. I don't know. I don't know. And now I haven't got a home to go to. No . . . I haven't got anywhere to go to on Christmas.

Dental technician M. looks at the blue flashing lights below

him. He's overwhelmed by a sad and terrible premonition that
he's going to do something horrible. Yes, I want to jump and put
an end to it all, M. thinks. But most of all, most of all . . . He
smiles to himself spitefully, I want to make my idiotic wife feel
sorry for once in her life. I want her to be tormented by remorse.
For the rest of her life. "He killed himself on Christmas because
I kicked him out." That's what she'll constantly say to herself as
she writhes in remorse.

M. steps over the railings with such a strong feeling of anger
and confidence that his ears are thumping and the blood is boil-
ing in his head.

So, I'm going to jump onto those cables and I'll be burnt to
a cinder, he thinks. He's very afraid but his anger is stronger.

He suddenly hears the screech of brakes behind him. A car
stops and reverses back a few yards. M. stands there waiting with
a foolish look on his face, one leg over each side of the railings as
if sitting on a horse. He turns back to look at the bridge and sees
two men getting out of a battered old Golf. They look younger
than him and a bit worse for wear. "What's up, my friend?" one
of them asks. M. is wondering whether to swing the other leg
over the railing and throw himself off the bridge, or wait for the
pair of annoying drunks to go away. "Nothing, I'm just sitting
here," M. mutters. "It's none of your business, so just fuck off."
"On the contrary, on the contrary, it is our business," the larger
of the two men nods. "Christmas suicides are our specialty. Are
they not?" he asks the other. The other takes a flat metal flask
out of his pocket, throws his head back and from a distance of
twenty centimeters precisely directs the stream of liquid into
his mouth. He swallows, hands the flask to his friend, and grabs
M. by the collar. With unexpected strength he gives him a sharp
tug and pulls him back to the other side of the railings. "So, let's
have a chat," he says. M. is suddenly overcome by such a sense
of confusion that his legs give away. "Who are you?" he asks.
"We're a rescue team," the taller one laughs and drinks. "You, my
friend, are probably one of those people who sink into depres-
sion at Christmas and other holidays. The sort of people whose
wives chuck them out of their homes and they decide to jump

off bridges, which is where we find them. Or isn't that right?" M. says nothing, just quivers because he's now overcome by fear, while all his feelings of anger and malice have dissipated. He stands silently staring at them. The tall one hands him the flat flask and says, "Drink!" M. drinks the cold, strong whiskey. It tastes very good. "Look, my friend," the short man takes the flask, "we don't want to interfere, but I'm sure that if you know a good place where you can go and get a drink and forget about your wife, until it blows over, you won't want to jump off anything. Am I right?" "I suppose so," M. says and bursts into tears. He sobs and covers his face with his hands. "Hurray!" The tall one rubs his hands. "This friend of ours really needs a drop. Here you are, have a quick drink, slug it down, my friend. For men, this is the best cure for tears." The tall man shoves the flask into M.'s hand. "It's like women and chocolate," the short one laughs. M. drinks and a moment later he's much calmer. The lump in his throat has gone, but his knees are still trembling a bit.

"Look, my friend," the short one leads him to the car, while the tall one tries to pee onto the high voltage cables under the bridge. "We're going to the seaside." "On Christmas?" M. says with a half-hearted expression of surprise. "Yes, oh yes!" The short one pushes him toward the car. "We're going to celebrate New Year's Eve there and have some innocent fun in the company of loose women and select drinks, happily and healthily, well at least more healthily than jumping off bridges onto railway lines. Well? What do you say?" "Can I call my wife?" M. asks. "Of course. Tell her you're going to a monastery. And don't forget to tell her that she's a miserable bastard, even though she's a lady. Ha, ha!" The short one opens the doors of the battered Golf. All three of them get in. The tall man drives, but so badly that M. feels afraid. They'll be the death of me, he thinks to himself. Then he remembers that ten minutes ago he was fully intending to kill himself and he laughs. They stop next to a phone booth. M. gets out and makes a call. When he puts the phone down, he feels so relieved that he wonders how he could have thought such things only half an hour previously. Who's the man in the house? Whose house is it and who's in the driver's seat? M. thinks to himself in delight.

Two Specific Cases

Blue Beard

A FEW DAYS after losing his most recent wife, Baron Blue Beard was feeling sad and lonely. He wanted a sweet, cheery woman by his side, and not to live a lonely and sad life like an old badger.

He set out on a quest around the villages and the estates of close and distant friends. He finally chose the daughter of an ordinary bourgeois, an honest man who had a small workshop for music boxes. The girl was as pretty as a rose in May. She had wondrously beautiful hair down to her waist.

Two weeks after Baron Blue Beard officially asked for the hand of Hilga (that was the girl's name), a huge, noisy wedding was arranged.

For the first week of their marriage, everything was like a fairy tale. Hilga chirruped like a little bird around her husband, astounded by the unseen luxury surrounding her.

She spent hours brushing her golden hair with a silver comb. She was truly proud of her wondrous and beautiful hair. She walked from room to room combing her hair with the silver comb.

On the tenth day of their wedding, Blue Beard found a long strand of fair hair in his tea. He smiled philosophically and removed it.

On the morning of the eleventh day, as he filled the wash basin, Blue Beard found a whole clump of long, fair hair which had fallen from her head as a result of her persistent combing. He just frowned but said nothing. All day long.

On the twelfth day he was horrified to find his favorite pointer, Max, choking and vomiting constantly. He put his hand down his throat and pulled out an incredibly long strand of fair hair. He let out a quiet, wheezing cry from deep in his chest. He grabbed the big spiked poker and ran to Hilga's room. She was sitting in front of the mirror slowly combing her hair. She gathered the hair which fell from her head into her hand, rolled them into balls, and casually cast them aside.

Blue Beard raised the poker and aimed a blow at her head, but stopped himself at the last moment. For a second, the images of his five previous wives flashed through his mind: Ruth, who snored; Gertrude, who shaved with his razor; Brunhilda, who put parsley in his cabbage; Luthen, who washed his red socks with his underwear; and Karin, who slurped her coffee loudly. "Why can't I be more restrained?" Blue Beard thought. "If I can't put up with my wives little foibles, then I'll have to live my entire life alone. And what's more, funerals are so expensive."

Blue Beard spun around on his heels. Hilga had not heard anything, she was so taken up with combing her hair. The Baron, first slowly and quietly, and then almost running, went to the bathroom in his chambers. He feverishly began to collect everything he needed: scissors, a razor, a bowl, a shaving brush, and shaving soap. Then humming a playful tune, he went back to Hilga's room.

Sleeping Beauty

Sleeping Beauty went into the pharmacy and ordered seven packets of Valium, four packets of Luminal, and three bottles of valerian drops. She also bought a special pillow with foam rubber points that massage the back of the head while you're asleep.

After the pharmacy she went to the book shop. She bought three very boring ladies' novels, very suitable for bedtime reading.

She then went into a shop for bed linen, where she bought a nightcap, soft flannelette pajamas, and a set of sheets, so soft and light that you want to go straight to bed and wrap yourself up in them.

From the electrical shop, she bought a bedside lamp with

soft, quivering glass fibres. It looked very beautiful and would help her get to sleep. She also bought a small ultrasound electric mosquito repellent for when she slept with the window open.

Finally, in an outburst of sentimentality, she bought herself a huge, soft, sweet, fluffy bear she could hug as she fell asleep.

"After all, I'm going to sleep for a hundred years. It's a very serious thing," Sleeping Beauty thought to herself.

She slowly walked back home. She had the nagging feeling that she had forgotten something important for her hundred-year sleep. The moment she got home, she made herself a coffee and sat down to think. She wanted to remember what she had forgotten. The thought that she had to get into bed made her feel anxious.

When she did get into bed and tried to read, she realized that she was trembling. She was trembling with nervous anxiety. The thought that she had to go to sleep and sleep for a hundred years wouldn't give her any peace. She decided to take a couple of pills and finally fall asleep. She didn't want to feel anxious any more.

She took almost an entire handful of sleeping pills, but she became frightened that she might have poisoned herself and she felt even more anxious. She went to the toilet to throw up. She went back to her room, but even the sight of her bed shocked her. She looked through the window. Everyone was asleep outside. Even the stray cats had gone into hiding places to sleep. She felt sad for herself. She started crying. Ever since she had been told that she was going to sleep for a hundred years, she had become so anxious that she couldn't sleep.

No. She hadn't slept a wink. She couldn't doze for a single moment. She had completely lost the ability to sleep. And so it went, for one hundred years . . .

The Case of the Necktie

You MIGHT REMEMBER the private detectives' club. It was about three hundred yards from the Hemus, where the tipsy prostitutes hang out during the night.

It was in this private detectives' club, now long gone, that Private Investigator Nesi Nestorov arranged his business meetings.

Nesi wasn't a bad detective. He was actually a journalist by profession. After about ten years spent at various second-rate newspapers, he decided to take life by the scruff of its neck. So he did the most stupid thing he had done in his life. He went from the frying pan into the fire. Actually it was much worse than that, it was like going from the frying pan into a camp fire somebody had pissed on to put it out. He earned a pittance as a private detective. To top it all, he had to work at night. That ruined his nerves, upset his stomach, and led to the complete destruction of his already half-destroyed family. Actually, Nesi was a complete loser. He never dressed smartly. He imagined that it made him look like Columbo. He looked like somebody who didn't buy his clothes, but stole them from a second-hand shop. The only things Nesi really insisted on were his neckties. He had about twenty of them. Most of them were very wide and colorful. 1960s-style. I suppose you could call them exotic.

One July evening, Nesi was sitting in the above-mentioned private detectives' club waiting for a business meeting.

I bet it's some fucking jealous wife again, he thought to himself. He was actually preoccupied with something else at that moment. He had been trying to find his favorite tie for the past week. It was purple with lemon-yellow rhomboids, or something like that. I bet my damned wife has hidden it on purpose! Nesi thought to himself. At that moment his thoughts were interrupted by a woman's voice, "Mr. Nestorov?" He could tell it was his client. Fat and evil, like my wife, the detective thought to himself sadly. He listened to her seemingly unending explanation. Yes, yes. It was a very sad business. Life and the World were like a pair of complete losers and nothing surprised Nesi. His client was exactly like Nesi had hopelessly imagined she would be. Stupid and jealous. She was the owner of some husband of whom she was idiotically jealous. Some vague female suspicions.

"So, I can count on you getting some photographs of my husband and that . . . woman he's been cheating on me with? I'll pay you when you give me the photographs? Is that right, Mr. Nestorov . . . Mr. Nestorov?"

The fat, jealous woman tapped him nervously on the shoulder. Nestorov was startled and looked at her with an expression of incomprehension. There was nothing about this woman that might rescue Nesi from the absolute frustration of life. She was constructed from the sort of banal atoms that nobody likes. During the entire time while she was describing her absurd suspicions, he had been thinking about his missing necktie. He had been imagining its wonderful, sour, fat, lemon . . . rhomboids, or whatever they were. "Yes, yes, the fee . . . You can pay me afterward," he muttered. "First, I'll get the photographs." "I want to ruin him, Mr. Nestorov," the woman croaked quietly and spitefully as they parted.

Investigating the sexual straying of the modern man was such a tedious, easy, and banal job. He sometimes thought it might be more interesting selling lottery tickets at the station. At least that way his life would be filled with more vivid impressions and passions, and he would never get bored.

For the next two days Nestorov followed the suspected husband as he took his normal routes. On the third day he was ready. He had a cheap camera and tape recorder in his pocket, so he could catch him in the little apartment where he obviously engaged in his insignificant extramarital dalliances.

The apartment was an attic room in Darvenitsa. Nestorov arrived by tram and waited for the man to appear. Nesi arrived in his battered Passat, parked in front of the apartment block, and hid behind a kiosk. It was a foolish thing to do. He had nobody to hide from. But he was shy and embarrassed by his own absurdity. He wasn't hiding from his target, just hiding. The world looked upon Nesi with disapproval, so he hid from it in shame.

Nestorov recognised the man from the back as he entered the block. He didn't look very closely. He had stopped taking an interest in the appearance of his victims. He waited for ten minutes and followed him. He arrived at the attic room. He put his ear to the door. He could hear a muffled conversation. Nesi waited for ten minutes and the conversation stopped. He heard a soft moaning sound. "Yes, now's the moment," the detective said to himself. He looked through the keyhole and saw that there was no key on the inside. Not even a key, or even the slightest desire to make the act of betrayal important or secret. He simply pressed quietly on the door handle and went in. The bathroom door was opposite the front door. He could hear the sound of running water. Clearly the first session of attic Bacchanalia was over and one of the adulterous participants was rinsing off the stains of bodily fluids. But as they washed off the bodily fluids and shame, they also washed off some of the meaning of what they were doing. It was something so natural.

Nesi crept quietly toward the door of the living room, straight ahead. He prepared his camera and tape recorder and hid in a small trash-filled alcove. He would wait for the person in the bathroom to come back into the room. Then he would jump out in his role as private detective, push the door open, and wait shamelessly with an icy smile on his face for the screams and yells and record them on the tape. Then with an air of annoyance he would run business-like down the stairs.

All this took place exactly as he had planned. The man came out of the bathroom and went into the bedroom. Nesi followed him. The man clumsily rolled onto the bed next to his lover. Nestorov raised his camera but his arms suddenly fell to his side and his body was overcome with a hot, prickly sensation.

The woman lying next to the clumsy, fat, hairy body of a man resembling an over-chewed stick of gum was Nestorov's very own wife. Ha!

The woman lay there waiting for the body to roll on top of her again. She lay there as the seconds passed slowly with pauses between them. She saw Nesi and pointlessly pulled the sheet up to her chin as she screamed silently. Unnaturally, somehow. Nesi stepped back, leant against the door, and tried to think of something. It occurred to him that his wife's legs were indecently fat and he wanted to cover them up. Then he took a deep breath, shook his head, and looked around the room. A filthy little room for betrayals. Suddenly his gaze fell upon the chair next to the bed. The man's clothes were hanging on the back of it. The filthy, wretched clothes of betrayal. On top of them lay something resembling a bright, poisonous reptile. Purple. And yellow.

His necktie!

The sad detective's wonderful necktie! It was lying on top of the crumpled clothes, also crumpled and still tied in a bad knot.

"So that's where it was!" For some reason Nesi felt a sense of extreme relief. It was a Sign and when people are given Signs, it means the Sender of the Signs is saying something to him. It didn't matter what. All the decisions he was to make from now on were a matter of his imagination. The wonderful imagination of the sad detective!

Nesi took two decisive steps forward, pushed the arm-waving man back into the bed and grabbed the wonderful necktie. He caressed its yellow rhomboids, put it into the pocket of his overcoat, and calmly left.

As he walked slowly down the stairs, he laughed with relief. When he got outside, he threw the camera and tape recorder into a garbage container and walked on, confident that he was ready to start a new and more meaningful life.

Christmas

D. WAS ALREADY old. His hair was thin and completely white, his skin was flabby. It hadn't yet acquired the parchment-like appearance of geriatric skin, but he had brown spots on his forehead and cheeks, and his neck resembled a succession of empty bags. His movements were still confident, although his hands trembled slightly when strained. He walked quickly, but out of habit, not because he wanted to walk quickly.

The disabilities of old age came upon him quietly, without startling him. Every morning with slight surprise he would notice a new one. He looked upon himself as a piece of fruit left out to dry and go to seed. The calmness with which he accepted his old age also surprised him. Sometimes he would even pat his yellow cheeks in front of the mirror with a sense of satisfaction. "Granddad," he would say as he shaved slowly and carefully.

He had become a widower three years ago. His wife had died slowly from chronic leukemia, without too much pain. They struggled for as long as they could with the illness, and then reconciled themselves to waiting for the end. His wife died a painless death at home. Her bodily organs just stopped. D. wasn't there at the very end, because he couldn't bear to look at her anymore, with her gaping mouth, her fidgeting hands, and rolling eyes. D. went to his dead wife when the doctor called for him. By now her face was calm. D. kissed her for the last time and sat down. He cried a little, and then got down to the task of organizing her funeral. This prevented him from feeling the dreadful emptiness.

For the past three years, D. had been alone. His only son,

estranged from him for some reason, went to America without any explanation. He called him on rare occasions, but they only exchanged meaningless pleasantries. D. had no friends. Who has friends at the age of sixty-six? In his life as an independent adult, D. had met many people, become close to some of them, parted from most of them, and only the closest had remained, but even they had melted away somewhere in the past. Some of them had died, others were still alive, but he never really seriously considered calling them. He even thought it a little humiliating to call an old friend, just because he was alone. So D. became accustomed to his loneliness, filling it with a carefully structured existence. He read books, did crosswords, and walked his dog, Sharo.

Sharo was a mongrel whom D. had found three months after his wife died. In the beginning, he felt nothing but pity for the small, filthy animal, but gradually they became attached to one another, in the same joyless way that old people become attached to each other. Sharo was old too.

Every day at six in the morning, two in the afternoon, and six in the evening, D. would take the dog out for an hour. He never put a leash on him, because Sharo was very obedient and so small and disheveled that it would have looked strange to have him on a leash like a Great Dane. While Sharo peed on the trees or just crouched because of his age, D. would look at the people and objects and notice small, previously unseen details. This gave him a sense of calm and tranquillity. D. was in generally good health. His heart beat rhythmically, his digestion was good, his thoughts were well organized and normal. He had learned to stifle any rare, accidental outbursts of emotion. Sometimes, with satisfaction, he would consider himself a well-balanced and moderate man.

D. considered moderation and wisdom synonymous.

One day D. noticed that winter had come. The third winter since his wife had died. One and a half years since he had been all alone except for Sharo. Over the past three years he had learned to cope with the winter, with his solitude, and with himself. He knew where to go, what to do, and what to think. In a world of chaos, D. had good and solid foundations: common sense and the belief that the World was fundamentally structured in the right way and if any of the minor details were to go wrong, they could be fixed. D. didn't believe in God, because he had never had to. He had never suffered very much and had never wanted for very much.

Christmas was coming. Ever since he had been alone, D. had spent Christmas alone in his warm slippers. His wife always hung a branch of a fir tree on his front door, and he did the same even though he shook his head in disapproval at his wife's superstitions. He would cook himself something. He wasn't a bad cook and he and Sharo would eat together. D. would make himself some tea and sit in his armchair. He would watch a little television, then put out the lights and go to bed, listening the distant beating of his heart.

That year, on Christmas Eve, D. went out at lunchtime to do some shopping. He walked around for a long time looking in the shops, but actually only bought a little piece of pork, a small sour cabbage, and a loaf of rye bread. He didn't need anything else. On his way home, he used his change to buy a small icon with a candle. For the past three years, he had always bought a Christmas present for the old, lonely concierge who accepted his gifts with tears in her eyes. It wasn't a deliberate attempt to make himself feel better, but he did, even though he didn't like pretense. He knew himself well and knew that this wasn't the way to become a better person.

On his way back to his old house in a side street in the center of the town, D. looked at the people and the things. He noticed that people were in a hurry and stressed. There were five times more things in the shops. Everyone was buying piles of things. D. noticed a beautiful young woman dressed in expensive and tasteless clothes coming out of a shop carrying a dozen gift boxes. A moment later D. saw a vagrant also burdened with his own baggage—shopping bags, boxes, and colored paper. D. walked by thinking that extremes are not actually extremes and that the differences between things are only superficial.

It was getting dark by the time he arrived back at his house.

He rang the concierge's bell and heard the sound of her aging footsteps. He took the present out of his pocket. She opened the door and her chin almost immediately began to tremble. Her eyes filled with tears. She took the brightly colored packet in both hands without looking to see what was inside. Through her tears she said how happy the little bit of attention made her feel, and how awful it was to be alone and she asked D. if he would like to come in. D. knew that the old woman would invite him in, because she always did, but he also knew that if he went in, he would have to sit on a hard chair in the half-dark listening to her monotonous complaints. She didn't have anything to offer him, and she only turned the lights on very rarely, because she was too poor. D. thanked her, wished her the best of health, and walked up to his apartment. Everything was in order. Like a little ball of dirty, gray wool, Sharo met him at the door. D. turned on the kitchen light and the unpleasant gloom disappeared. The window became a deep-blue color. D. hated the darkness. He switched on the little television on top of the fridge and started cooking. He moved in measured steps back and forth like an old man who had had enough time to hone the finer points of his movements. Within one hour he had finished cooking. He put the dirty dishes into the sink, placed a plate, knife, and fork for himself on the table, and put Sharo's bowl on the ground. He looked around, everything was in order. He opened a bottle of red wine, which he had bought a week earlier, poured himself a glass, and took a sip. When his wife was alive, D. used to drink a glass or two on occasion. Now he only drank at Christmas. As the large sip of wine slowly trickled down into his stomach, he began to feel slightly lightheaded. He served the meal to himself and the dog and they began to eat. D. dried his mouth with a napkin, just because it was Christmas. His wife always insisted on this. She knew how to fold napkins for special occasions.

D. looked at the cupboard where the picture of his wife was hanging. He tried to recall what she had looked like when she was young, to create a clear image in his mind, but he couldn't. D. bowed his head and looked into his plate. A decent plate with a blue edge, as old as he was. A lump came into D.'s throat and he drank another glass of wine. He looked again at his wife's picture. It didn't resemble anything he knew. Suddenly he felt as though he was suffocating and the blood began to pulsate in his ears. He was a lonely old fool, playing the role of a calm man who accepted life calmly and without fear. Nobody would call him, nobody would think about him, even death itself would ignore him, since he was in good health. Yes, he had led a good life, and now he was healthy, well-balanced, and moderate. He was overcome by terror. It was like waking from a deep sleep only to be hit by the nightmare of waking reality. He looked again at the picture of his wife. Who was she? A woman he didn't know! He knew her shoe size, the mole on her back, the scent of her hair. But he didn't know her, and couldn't remember what he did with her. They had lived together. He could remember dates, but they were only empty names of dates. There must have been happy and unhappy moments, but D. couldn't remember, since he was alone now and he must be alive, since he could feel the entire terrible lava of life rising in his throat. He drank more wine, but it didn't calm him. He felt a terrible anger against the world that had deceived him and now left him alone. He began to sense a dreadful hatred for his life, for Life itself, for the life he had lived so carefully and confidently, as if it had all been leading to a wonderful culmination. D. looked around the kitchen. It was empty and the dog was lying scared on the floor.

D. got up and pressed his forehead on the cold glass of the window. The world outside was teeming with life deceiving more and more people. Millions of people flitted before D.'s eyes. They confidently and without a shadow of doubt accepted the promises life made to them. It was Christmas and people were drinking, laughing, crying, exchanging best wishes, and hoping. D. stood in his empty kitchen. His fists were clenched in powerless anger.

An open-topped car passed by under D.'s window. There were a dozen or so people sitting in it. They had opened the roof so that they could make as much noise as they could. Young women, young men. The women screamed joyfully and the men were holding bottles. Loud music boomed out of the car. D. turned away from the window. The dread that suddenly filled the little kitchen stunned him. His wife was looking down spitefully and mockingly from the picture on the wall. The dog was curled up in the farthest corner. The bloody knife he had used to cut the meat was still lying on the work surface in the kitchen. D. stood stunned and motionless for about a minute. Then a quiet and evil gurgle began in his chest. It became louder and louder, until it erupted into an inhuman roar. D. bared his teeth, there was nothing left of the decent old man. The veins on his neck and forehead swelled, his eyes narrowed and began to spin. D. grabbed the table with the remains of the Christmas meal on it and turned it over. Then he grabbed the bloody knife from the sink, and with a muffled roar he ran outside into the dark winter night.

Nevermore

He was woken by the constant buzzing in his head and the tightness in his throat. Purple spots, golden flies, and an unpleasant dark-red veil danced and played strangely in front of his eyes. That's what always happens about four hours after drinking the first bottle of cognac. A familiar nausea and increased heart rate affect the upper half of the body, while the lower part is stiff and weak.

He raised his old cognac-filled head, which encountered the sudden solidity of the complete darkness. This solidity appeared suddenly out of nowhere, causing sparks to glitter before his eyes. His head ached, both back and front. Bizarrely, from somewhere behind his eyelids, the memory of his grandfather's funeral surfaced. He remembered it raining, the gravediggers throwing lumps of mud onto the coffin, which fell with a thud. His grandmother sobbed calmly and rhythmically as she held onto the waist of one of his aunts. The memory was clear and there was something reassuring about it.

He raised his head again, more carefully this time. It didn't hit anything, just knocked gently against something. Something as hard as stone, because it probably was a stone. He was overcome by fear. An indefinable hot wave flowed over him from his feet to his face. Sweat ran from his temples, his groin, and down his back. Hot sweat on a hot body. A terrible thought occurred to him—that he was hanging in midair trying to step onto the ground. His head thumped against the hard, idiotic ground above him.

11:25 A.M.

The flesh of his stomach shivered, the insides of his stomach shivered, and his hands trembled. What the hell was wrong with his hands, let's just see if they're trembling or not. How good it was to have a whole day without alcohol. His chest swelled with a feeling of joy. A lump came to his throat. It was a spasm, not one of joy, but pleasant all the same. It was a proud spasm of his triumph over his will. The professor took one hand in the other and checked his pulse. 78, that was excellent. He touched his forehead, there was no sweat. He looked at the woman sitting hunched over opposite him. It occurred to him that there was nothing sadder than a woman sitting hunched over, waiting outside a psychiatrist's consulting room. It also occurred to him that there was no achievement greater and prouder than his triumph over alcohol. He was a man of courage, hostile to everyone, a man of steel will who had not touched alcohol for an entire day. Despite this, he was not rolling around on the floor, he wasn't kicking his legs up in the air, and he wasn't biting people. He was just a little anxious, but that was natural.

His face quivered in a nervous, silent, and completely involuntary laugh. What utter nonsense, utter nonsense. I'm a little tense . . . But that's normal . . . I have to behave calmly in front of the doctor. Here I am, Doctor, a completely calm, slightly bored man, who doesn't have the slightest interest in your help. I've come to see you only because I like you. I don't drink. I might have drunk, but that's only because I like alcohol. So . . . how are you, Doctor? You don't look too well. You should quit smoking while you're young. Look after the ticker. There's absolutely nothing wrong with me, no, cold turkey. Alcoholics go through cold turkey as well, don't they? What cold turkey are we talking about? Are you going through it as well? There you are, I'm getting worked up again. I have to be completely calm and relaxed. I have to let the doctor ask the questions. I have to answer in a cool polite manner. Why don't I take a diazepam, just in case.

The professor held his head in his hands, breathed slowly and measured his pulse. It was 85. He needed to stop thinking. Thinking makes you anxious and the brain kills the body.

The doctor appeared at the door. He made a hook out of his index finger and invited the professor to enter the consulting room. He got up slowly and tried to resemble the person who was invited to lecture on linguistics at the University of Boston. He stumbled, putting an end to any similarity to a person who lectures at the University of Boston. That damned vestibular apparatus, damned brain, damned doctor who notices every stumble. He entered the consulting room and sat on the miserable couch. Everything in the room was miserable. On the wall there was a miserable, crooked, yellow picture. There was a little perspiration on his forehead, but that was normal, it was summer after all.

1:20 P.M.

"Two bottles of cognac and a pack of Shipkas," the professor said and tried to make his voice sound like a person who was buying cognac for guests. For a huge dinner party of sober-minded individuals who pour just one finger into short-stemmed glasses.

The consultation had gone well. The doctor made him touch the tip of his nose with his index finger, stand upright, barefoot, in a variety of humiliating poses with the toes of the left foot touching the heel of his right. The doctor was talking to some woman on the telephone. He shouted at her a little, then he turned to ask the professor if he was still drinking and when was the last time he had had a drink. "I haven't had a drop since last Friday, not a drop for more than five days," the professor lied and looked into the doctor's eyes, as everybody does who wants to lie convincingly. "Well done." The doctor wrote him a prescription for tegretol which could be bought over the counter without a prescription and he said he was very happy for him. "That's a great achievement. I'm really pleased. It's a great achievement." The professor felt reassured, "I hope you had no doubts, Doctor?" He left the room with the step of a man who still might receive an invitation to lecture in Boston. He measured his pulse as he left the room. It was calm and measured, and his breathing was slow. Everything is in a person's brain, in his psyche. The brain supports the body, the brain makes it indestructible. The body needs the occasional drink. The will squeals in displeasure and needs to be fed.

"Two bottles of cognac and a pack of Shipkas."

1:27 P.M.

The boulevard in front of the clinic was being dug up. The workers were standing in yellow mud at the bottom of the trench, three yards below street level. They weren't digging, but leaning on their spades looking at the mud. Smoky exhaust billowed out of the roaring excavator, annoying everyone. The excavator driver said something rude, stopped the engine, and climbed down the steep slope into the hole. He went to look at something and spat at nothing in particular. There were wide, gaping, cement sewer pipes at the bottom of the hole.

The professor raised his head toward the sky and took a huge swig right there and then as he was standing at the edge of the hole. A drop landed on his forehead. It was a strange and unnatural drop, as if somebody had spat on him. Then other drops followed, making huge dark spots on the yellow mud. It smelled good, like wet dust. "I have to find shelter, somewhere I can drink while the rain patters on the roof above me," the professor said to himself.

The workers collected their tools and slowly made their way to an old, battered, smelly, bright-blue van. At least that's how the professor imagined it looked, since he couldn't see one nearby. The cement sewer pipes were almost completely darkened by the huge rain drops and they lay dark-blue against the yellow background at the bottom of the excavation. "That's where I'll sit and drink, hidden from the stupid rain pouring down on top of me. The cognac will soften my stiff legs and make me think about fragrant mountain meadows and women under the age of twenty-five bathing in mountain dew," the professor said to himself.

1:58 P.M.

It had grown pleasantly dark outside. Some of the cars had their
headlights on. The professor stuck his head out of the pipe and
looked at them. They were up above him and it seemed strange
to him that he was down below while they were up above, but
all the same everything seemed to be in order. The consultation
had gone well, the cognac was a little warm, but it was all right,
he had matches and cigarettes and everything was in order. It was
strange and pleasant. He slid a little farther inside the pipe where
it was warmer and darker. Through a little hole he could see a
very small bit of the sky—a poplar tree with yellow-green leaves
trembling, or barely trembling, against the blue background of
the sky. He took a big swig and smiled at the good things that
had happened to him. The alcohol trickled pleasantly down his
throat, causing a slight burning sensation and a not-unpleasant
acid reflux. He looked back at the poplar tree with its trem-
bling-not-trembling, yellow-green leaves. There was something
nice about all of this both inside him and outside him. He leaned
back against the pipe and began slowly to rub his head left-to-
right and then right-to-left. The short hair on the back of his
head produced a pleasant springing sensation. He felt sleepy.

10:50 P.M.

The professor crept on his hands and knees for about five minutes but couldn't find any aperture leading to the outside world.
He began panting, overcome by a presentiment of terror. He lit
a match and looked at his watch. It was 10:55. He must have
slept for nine whole hours.

His knees, elbows, his entire body was convulsed with terror,
the herald on a purple horse presaging the onset of panic. He
sat down and lit a cigarette. He breathed deeply for about two
minutes and tried to think soberly. Soberly! He felt like shit. He
had lost it all and his breath stank of undigested alcohol. "What
a failure! What a failure! I've ruined everything now! I must have
rolled over while I was sleeping. I'm simply not crawling in the
right direction."

He sat for about a minute and calmed himself down. Then

he rubbed his knees and elbows and crawled in the opposite direction. He crawled and crawled.

For six minutes, then eight, and then another ten minutes. The darkness oppressed him and closed in on him! Where should I go? Forward along the pipe? Did he have a choice? No.

He crawled ahead mechanically, unconsciously, and silently. The professor sweated, snorted, and occasionally groaned. Finally he sat down and screamed. Just in his mind. It's terrifying to scream in complete darkness and complete solitude. At a depth of two or three yards under the ground, he thought to himself. All he could see was the red circles of complete darkness.

"So I've been buried alive, that's a fine state of affairs. Oh my god! Fuck, fuck, fuck!"

He punched, kicked, and pushed his head, back, thighs, nose, and stomach at the ceiling of the pipe. It wasn't very wide now. It had become very narrow. As narrow as a coffin. Narrower than a coffin, the professor thought to himself. The first thought that went through his head was, Why didn't people suffer from claustrophobia in their clothes? Clothes are terribly tight and restrictive.

He pulled off his tie and tore it. He wrapped it around his fist and began thumping more calmly and more methodically on the ceiling. The roof of my last home, he thought to himself. The absurd calmness and rhythm of what he was doing brought about an even greater sense of terror. What on earth am I doing, for God's sake, I'm bricked in here. Nobody's going to hear me.

There was something sticking out of the inside pocket of his jacket. He touched it and felt something round. He pulled it out and grinned with pleasure. The feeling of satisfaction a condemned man experiences when he smokes his last cigarette. The satisfaction of the immured man when he drinks his last swig of cognac. A lot of swigs, a whole bottleful.

10:56 P.M.
"Save the matches, fool!"

10:59 P.M.

". . . I'm getting on well with the bottle, and the alcohol's helping me. I feel calmer now. I've lived a stupid life. I feel sorry for my daughter, but she doesn't need me anyway. What have I done with my stupid, fucking stupid, wasted life."

11:07 P.M.

"I have to leave at least ten matches and I must have at least a third of a pint left. I'm not going to give up. I'm going to crawl and I'll die crawling. I like crawling. I'm a snail. I like crawling. I like creeping and drinking. I love drinking and crawling." He crawled slowly and persistently, while muttering through his nose, groaning calmly and rhythmically. His groans resembled a Japanese fisherman's song. He crawled for about two hours.

SATURDAY, 1:12 A.M.

"Ilovecrawlingilovecrawlingilove . . . crawling."

He crawled for about another half an hour and stopped. "Oh, fuck, fuck, fuck!"

He drank some cognac, which burned his stomach, throat, and heart like lighted coals. For the first time in years he wanted to drink water.

Water!!!!

1:30 A.M.

"Rats. Bad rats. They frighten me to death. Yuck . . . They don't frighten me at all. I'm dying here bricked inside this pipe and I'm frightened of rats. Why do people, when they know they're going to die anyway, sooner or later, get frightened by stupid things, and try to achieve stupid things, and why bother washing, if you know you're going to die? Why bother cutting your nails? Why do stupid things? What's the point of being frightened of snakes and unemployment? We're all going to die anyway? Shit! I only like crawling. Drinking and crawling!"

1:35 A.M.

"I'm going to die."

1:40 A.M.

"The crawling's going really well. I'm really good at it. I'm good at everything I do. I once saved a man from drowning. I was young, and there was this man who was drowning. I grabbed him and swam for about half a mile with him and saved him. I swam well. Yes, yes, yes! I can save somebody today as well. I just need a little cognac and somebody to love me. I don't need anything else. I just need to crawl."

2:30 A.M.

"I'm not going to crawl anymore."

4:32 A.M.

"I'm still crawling. There's nothing else left. I have to do something. What's that strange noise up above? Oh my God! It's a tram. Fuck, fuck, fuck! Where are there trams nearby? Three yards above me. It's close. No, it has to be a tram. It must be the Levski Monument. I have to crawl."

5:50 A.M.

"My knees are cut to the bone. They're right down to the bone. What's the next stage of this trauma? Bone marrow. My knees are worn to the bone marrow. I have to keep on crawling. It's easy now. The pipes are going down. I'm going in the same direction. I could be near Poduyane. Perhaps I'll die in Poduyane. That's where I was born."

5:59 A.M.

"Or Orlandovtsi! I don't know. I'll just crawl and wait calmly for death."

7:31 A.M.

"There's light in the darkness . . . There it is . . . light, and I can hear noise. Ha! Ha, ha, ha! I can see the world on the other side of the yellow mud. The pipe ends here and there's a world outside . . . Ha! I'm so happy, so happy. I want to cry, I feel sorry for myself, sorry for my life. I'm saved, I'm so happy. There's a slope of yellow mud. I'll crawl up it. Why should I? I'll crawl up it. Why should I? I'll crawl . . ."

7:33 A.M.

There were old women hunched over, dressed in black, standing at the stop waiting for a tram. Yes, it was Orlandovtsi. The cemetery. The professor dragged himself out of the mouth of the pipe, waddled slowly over to the tram stop and sat down on a covered bench. The old women looked at him. He put his hand in his pocket and took out the bottle. It had two fingers of brown liquid left in it. He raised the bottle and drank it. Then he raised the collar of his jacket around his neck and shoved his hands under his armpits. Because it was a cold, wet morning.

Orange, Almost Brown

HE LIVED IN Izgrev and everything in his life was fine. Even his work, which in our day is quite incredible, especially if you're a freelance artist. He sold a couple of paintings every month for an average of five hundred dollars each. Not a bad amount. He held exhibitions with a group of friends who were young and moderately avant-garde, i.e., they still used canvases and paints, rather than roadkill cats and varying shades of green. He was even more moderately avant-garde. Not only did he use canvases and paints, he wasn't very extravagant in his choice of paints. He always painted in the same blue-gray spectrum, if such a shade could be said to exist. He just couldn't stand brightly coloured daubing. He considered the use of a wide spectrum of colors to be a senseless and lunatic display of gypsy vulgarity. He had felt this way since he was a child.

While the other children liked to wear red track suits and yellow shell suits with blue stamped lettering, he liked to dress in a brown sweatshirt and dark-blue, completely neutral-colored, trousers. Everything he had was either gray, blue, or brown. Ever since he was little, he liked graphics. He was interested in the idea of the missing shade, and that if color was added to it, it might ruin everything. He began painting with restrained colors such as gray, brown, and blue. Even black annoyed him with its vividness.

Despite this strange passion for indifferent shades, he was quite talented and things were going well for him. He was successful with his pictures and everything else in his life. He was talented in his life as well.

There was one thing that bothered him. His wife. No, not his wife. She was quite wonderful . . . Well, not exactly wonderful . . . she was very beautiful, artistic, emotional . . . and whatever else they say about women who drive you crazy and play on your nerves. She was a very interesting woman, isn't that what they say about women you want to slap across the backside with your belt? She was so artistic that she used to wear a tiny flower pot around her neck with a real pansy in it. She not only had a navel piercing and an ankle bracelet, but also a ring on each of her toes. He could accept that. He was eccentric as well. However, his painful sensitivity to vivid colors screamed out in horror whenever she put on bright-orange makeup and dyed her hair bright green.

She was a ceramic artist and made things out of clay, but it wasn't the clay that interested her. After she fired her chalices in the kiln in their shared studio, the real work would begin. She covered the wretched but pleasantly brown clay with screaming, sinister, brilliant but terrifying, life-affirming colors. That's what she would do.

This didn't make him angry, since it didn't impinge profoundly on his personal life. And for a long time it *didn't* impinge on his personal life. Until one day it did.

The first thing she did was paint the window frames in the kitchen yellow. He screamed quietly, inside himself. He couldn't take it, and a week later he repainted them brown. Only then did he calm down. After all, the kitchen was the place they ate! But then she grew restless. She painted the chairs violet. He gnashed his teeth for two days and finally threw them out. He bought some plastic garden chairs, which were at least white. Then she began a campaign in the other rooms. She put her gaudy ceramics all over the place, hung macramé, and covered the walls and floors with vivid embroidered rugs, even the ceiling. All this made him feel dizzy. He felt nauseous and his head was filled with vague thoughts of revenge. From the moment they met until now, they had never had a serious argument. She was just so preoccupied with her orange lipstick and violet hair dye, not to mention the artificial rubies on her toes, that they never quarreled. Sometimes, for the mere sake of it, they would have the occasional spat. Until now.

One day, however, he decided it was time they had an argument. He told her quite directly how much he hated bright colors. "I don't want any more bright colors, at least not in my personal space! Do you understand?!" he told her. "Don't talk to me like that . . . it's my personal space as well. I can't live in . . . look at this place . . . it's more like a cave . . ." she replied.

The next day, he stood in the studio simmering with cold fury. She was an idiot. Everything she did was probably aimed at annoying him. Scratching with her orange nails at his hypersensitive perception of color.

He came home at ten o'clock in the evening. It was dark in the apartment. He lit all the lights in their big living room. He let out a completely normal, piercing, but horrified scream. The living room, like all normal living rooms, had four walls. However, each of them was a different color—yellow, orange, pink, and bright blue. She was sitting in her armchair, which was covered (along with the sofa and the other armchairs) in some kind of monstrosity with a bright check pattern.

He went over to her. He smiled. She didn't notice that his smile concealed something that shouldn't have been there. He bent down and closed his eyes as if to kiss her. She smiled stupidly and stretched her face toward his. Then he began slowly, persistently, and calmly to strangle her.

Half an hour later he had turned on the kiln in the studio and was stuffing her lifeless body into it. The last part of her body to go into the kiln was her left hand with its lemon-yellow fingernails. The kiln worked all night long. At half past eight in the morning he swept about three pounds of ashes out of the bottom of the kiln into a dustpan. The ashes were an extremely pleasant shade of gray brown with a slight nuance of blue.

Suddenly an idea occurred to him that brought a smile to his face. He smiled, and in his smile there was something bluish brown. He put the beautiful ashes in a brown paper bag and went back toward the Izgrev district to his apartment. He stopped at Pioneer Station on his way and bought a big can of white emulsion paint and some paint rollers. He went into the apartment, looked angrily at the brightly painted walls, and opened the paint can. He dipped a long brush into it. Then he took the packet of beautiful gray-brown ashes out of his pocket. He poured them in the can and began stirring until he got the desired color. He had never before achieved such a perfect color in any of his paintings!

Love

THE FISH CAME out onto the shore and flopped down. Its fins were stiff with exhaustion. The physical effort had been so great that even its swim bladder quivered and its smooth, scaly body trembled unceasingly. It had swum without stopping for a whole week. Now that it had reached its goal, it could rest. It began to fall asleep. At least it's warm and dry here on the bank . . . it thought. And fell asleep.

Evening was approaching in the Medical Academy's Faculty of Microbiology, and it was getting dark. On Volgograd Boulevard—or Levski as it had recently been renamed, but the name doesn't really matter—there was a column of nervous, noisy cars, all rushing to some seemingly important destination. It was stuffy and gloomy in the Faculty, it hadn't occurred to anybody to turn on the fluorescent lights. Students lazily paced back and forth in one of the bigger laboratories. They were clearly annoyed at having to waste their evening seeding microbes in agar. Most of them were probably thinking about seeding their own genetic material in a suitable place. A very young and pretty assistant who looked exciting when seen from the front, and pleasant when seen from the back, was sitting on a swivel stool drinking coffee from a laboratory beaker. From time to time she stole a glance at the broad back of student S., and secret little feminine thoughts flitted through her mind.

S. was in a bad mood. He paid absolutely no attention to the swivel stool. He was searing a microbiological needle in a flame, and then cooling it again. He stirred up various test tubes, then placed various cocci and bacteria in petri dishes, and from time to time secret little masculine thoughts flitted through his mind.

About two months previously, something quite banal had happened between the pretty assistant and S. They had left work together one evening and instead of going their separate ways, they had gone to a pleasant open-air cafe in Tsar Boris Park. They drank a little vodka, talked a lot, held hands, got a little excited with each other, and went to S.'s apartment. All night long until morning they did those things students and assistants do together at night, the things all men and women in the world do when they're alone together and naked. The very next day, S., who was essentially an aloof and incomprehensibly cold young man, began to behave in such a cold, vulgar, and offensive way that the pretty young assistant made frequent visits to the Faculty toilets to cry. After that she seemed to feel better. God only knows what happens in the heads of pretty young assistants.

Actually, looking at things through the dispassionate eyes of a third-person observer, she was in love with this vulgar, gloomy, and incomprehensible young man. He was handsome and very clever, but there was something vague and slightly threatening about him. He looked like a man with a hand grenade in his pocket. However, it wasn't his outward appearance or his clever and sometimes mocking words that were important. Women sometimes fall in love without any reason.

It was almost completely dark by now. Still, nobody had thought of turning on the lights. S. suddenly dropped a petri dish. It fell to the floor and shattered. The assistant was startled out of her tightly woven forest of thoughts and even got up from her swivel stool. But she didn't go anywhere near his bench. He knelt down and picked up the shards of glass in such a way that he didn't have to turn toward her, going out of his way to deliberately turn his back to her. He cut himself on one of the shards, muttered something, and, still hunched over and not looking to either side, he went into a side room containing countless test tubes and dishes with colonies of all sorts of terrible bacteria and spirochetes to get some gauze and disinfectant. It's not a good idea to cut yourself in a microbiology laboratory. If you do get

a cut, you have to disinfect it with great care. The first-aid cupboard stood next to an oven-looking device used to incubate
microbes. At that moment it was rather calmly holding some test
tubes of *Bacillus botulinus*—an extremely dangerous bacillus that
produced such an unimaginably strong toxin that the smallest
amount could kill dozens of people.

A moment later, S. returned from the side room with a ban-
daged finger. As he passed by the assistant, a faint smile appeared
on his face, but he didn't look at her. He reacted as if an old
newspaper in a plastic bag or a forgotten box of orange juice
was there on the stool. It made her so sad that she, too, turned
away. She bit one of her pretty little nails. S. sat at his bench.
He opened a book and began to read. What a rude bastard he is.
Everything about him is rude. He looks unhinged, perhaps he is,
or perhaps I just don't understand him. I hate him. I can't stand
him. He doesn't want to look at me. He's arrogant. I'm stupid.
Why do I like him so much? the assistant thought to herself.

When the test was over, a Greek student from Thessaloniki
went over to the swivel stool and began in a long-winded way to
explain something in bad Bulgarian with an annoying lisp. She
wasn't listening to him. She was staring anxiously at S.'s back as
he gathered up his things and stuffed them into his backpack. He
shook hands with his colleagues and then arrogantly and rudely
walked toward the door and left. The assistant couldn't take it
anymore. She turned her face to the Greek student with such a
look of annoyance that he stopped in mid-lisp. She pushed the
stool back and quickly grabbed her bag. "Goodbye, I'll see you
all on Thursday," she said in a tense voice without looking at
anybody. She stood pensively for a few seconds.

She went to the little side room, where she stood for a
moment in thought, then looked around, washed her hands,
and quickly left the Faculty. Outside in the boulevard it was by
now completely dark. Cars rushed by left and right. Pedestrians
resembling anxious ghosts in the evening passed her by. The assistant walked up the road toward the Levski Monument with
tiny, tense footsteps. She hoped. A sense of bitter excitement
filled her heart. She wanted to catch up with S. "I just hope he

hasn't caught the trolley bus," she thought. After walking about a hundred steps staring at her feet, she looked up. S. was about ten yards in front of her. He was walking slowly, strangely, in a somehow offensively calm way. The assistant caught up with him and softly, but decisively tapped him on the shoulder. He turned around, looked at her for a moment, but his face revealed no emotion. "Hello," he said in a calm voice, as though greeting an acquaintance he hadn't seen for six months. The assistant trembled with disappointment, which she had been expecting. "I want to sit down and talk to you for a while. Really. Just for a while." S. looked at her, then scratched one of his eyebrows and said, "Sure, all right then." They walked on. They walked slowly without talking, but as happens with people who aren't talking but thinking about some other important thing, they imperceptibly began to increase their pace. They soon reached Tsar Boris Park. They hadn't exchanged a single word. It was as though somebody else was leading them. They reached the small cafe where they had found themselves two months ago. They sat down and said nothing for two more minutes. Then she got up suddenly and looked at him, "What would you like to drink? A beer, perhaps?" "Sure." "Great, I'll have a beer too," she said with a tense note in her voice. She went to the bar. They were sitting at the darkest and most distant table. A minute later she brought the beers back to their dark, distant table. On the way back she stopped and put the glasses down on an empty table. She rummaged around in her pocket. Nobody was looking at her. She took out a long, narrow object. It was a test tube. She tipped its contents into one of the glasses. Then she quickly went back to S. He was sitting there with a calm expression on his face. She was calm too. However, there was also something unfamiliar about her calm. She put the glasses on the table and sat down. They continued to sit in silence and she looked at him through narrowed eyes. Her jaw muscles seemed constantly to tighten and relax. Suddenly he leaned over to her. He wasn't looking at her. He bent down completely and laid his head on her hand. She trembled but didn't push him away. She felt a warm liquid on the palm of her hand. "What's wrong?" she wanted to ask, but the words wouldn't come out of her mouth. Then S. slowly raised his head, looked at her with tears in his eyes and mumbled something. "What, what did you say?" he wanted to ask, but the words wouldn't come out of his mouth. Then he tried to speak again, but choked. He cleared his throat and said quietly, "I said that I love you very much. But for the past two months you've been so terribly cold toward me. I can't understand you and I'm embarrassed to talk to you. I get the feeling that every time I walk past you, you're laughing at me. What's going on? Why are you treating me like this? Do you find me so repulsive?" She looked at him in the way a mouse looks at a python. She was frightened, very frightened. She looked at him for a moment, then jumped up, grabbed his glass, and disappeared somewhere into the darkness. About a hundred yards away she stopped at a trash can. She was awkwardly carrying the glass at arm's length in front of her. She put it on the ground and took a plastic bag out of her pocket. She had stowed the bag away for the moment when the glass would be empty. She carefully picked up the glass, placed it in the bag, and tied it up. Then she put it very carefully into the trash can. I just hope a bum doesn't find it, she thought, "botulin is a terrible thing." Then she went quickly back to the cafe. She walked up to the bar and ordered another beer. She went back to the dark, distant table. She sat down, leaned over, and kissed S. on the hand. "How on earth could you not have realized that I love you so much? Yes, yes. You're crazy. But I love you so much." He looked at her and said nothing. His eyes were red. She stroked his face. She was very calm. "I went to get you another beer. That one looked a bit off to me. At least that's what I thought . . . Cheers! You can smile now!"

Tired of Understanding

ANTON K. UNDERSTOOD that he had been born when he was four years old. His parents had understood this fact four years earlier.

Anton K. didn't care what his parents had understood, because his own four-and-a-half-pound head was full of other things, which caused him concern. He wasn't even concerned about his newly erupted teeth, which had begun to decay almost immediately after they appeared.

In this alien and unpleasant World of which Anton K. timidly hoped to be the center, there were too many Things to Be Understood. He didn't want to understand everything (who does?), just those things in the World that annoyingly entered his four-and-a-half-pound head through his ears, eyes, nose, and the tips of his fingers and other apertures of the soul.

One of the first things that Anton K. wanted to understand was the mystery of his own excrement. At the age of four, he didn't know that this was the first thing that most children are interested in. He hid under his bed to let go of a few turds and then poked about in them. He smelt them and tasted them. It was disgusting but at the same time very enticing. It was then that Anton K. realized, rather than understood, that many of the most attractive things in life are also disgusting. And vice versa.

Anton K. had a caring, but completely distant and vague mother. He didn't love her, because he still didn't know how that was done. But when he was separated from her, he experienced a sense of mortal anxiety (is this love?). For months, four-year-old Anton K.'s mother wondered where the smell of excrement was coming from. When she found his secret piles, she lost her temper, cleaned them up, and scolded him mercilessly. Then Anton K. realized that he would never experience the pleasure of understanding something without hiding and paying a price for it. The price of humiliation, for example.

Anton K.'s mother was rough. Life had deprived her of any human appearance she might once have had. Anton K. would have to live for many more years with people, in order to understand that persistent and monotonous living turned people into dry, heartless, angry mummies wrapped in rags according to the season, and motivated by vague, uninteresting mechanisms. It would take years for Anton K. to understand that life would do the same to him.

So Anton K. found out what shame and pain were. They were inflicted on him by the person who claimed to love him most in this world. After some brief, shapeless, infantile reasoning, he concluded that people, by nature, are bad.

At the age of about five, when he began to meet other children, Anton K. discovered that these other children—like him but with other parents, who he had noticed treated them kindly—were evil creatures without a drop of mercy.

Based on the evidence of his friends, Anton K. concluded that children were capable of doing all kinds of disgusting things, from burning cockroaches on the kitchen stove to murdering another human being. He became convinced of this when he was about seven years old. It happened one day when his friends in the neighborhood removed all his clothes and forced him to stand completely naked in front of a group of girls. As he stood there naked and terrified with shame, the boys beat him with sticks until he bled. Then they stole his cheap little toy ball and gleefully cut it up with a pocket knife. They did it without any obvious reason. Other than for some incomprehensible joy.

More years would have to pass for Anton K. to understand that senseless cruelty is one of the main forms of enjoyment for people.

The ball that his friends cut up was a present to Anton K. from his parents. It was a wretched little ball bought without any particular thought for his seventh, sad (as they normally were) birthday. The ball wasn't any good, and very cheap.

Anton K.'s parents thought that it wasn't good for children to have good things. They believed that good things spoiled children. Anton K. had heard them say this.

He had also seen spoiled, mouldy cheese. He imagined that if children had good things, they would get spoiled and mouldy like the cheese.

At that time (like at all other times) possessions were the most important thing for the self-esteem of any child. There was always some proud little child who would ride past the others on his new bike, screech to a halt beaming with pride, and expect everybody else to admire it. And everybody else did admire it. Another child would go on a trip abroad in Daddy's new car, staring ahead with neck outstretched, not even looking back to wave at his friends. With a lump of excitement in his throat, he knew that everybody else was jealous. And everybody else *was* jealous. Most of all, Anton K. was jealous.

Anton K.'s parents didn't want to spoil him. That's why he was always dressed in old clothes handed down from his older cousins (so he would learn to appreciate the little things). He couldn't invite his friends home because his mother didn't allow it. If he did take someone back home secretly, his mother would immediately appear out of nowhere and throw them out in the most humiliating way possible. Thanks to the efforts of his parents to keep him from growing up spoiled, Anton K. wasn't spoiled. He grew up depressed, spiteful, and envious without understanding why.

So, at the age of seven, Anton K. was ashamed of his cheap little ball and his worn-out hand-me-down clothes. Nevertheless, his ball had been a present. He loved it and would even hug it now and then, because he hoped it would love him back. He wanted to be able to love his parents in the same way, but he couldn't.

So when his friends cut up his little ball, Anton K. shut himself in his room and cried for two whole days. Then he understood that things like that would happen to him frequently, and he began to prepare himself.

He also understood that he would have to hate the people around him quietly and secretly, but also that he would have to acquiesce to them because they were stronger than him, and they were stronger than him because they were more malicious. Anton K. wanted to become more malicious, but it was too late!

When you don't show something at the right moment, it's better never to show it at all. He understood this after he got punched in the mouth a few times, because he had tried to stand up for himself.

It was then that Anton K. discovered the following: the weaker you are, the more you will be humiliated, hated, and tormented by others. He understood, also, that when you are weak, you will be blamed for all the bad things you've done and all the bad things the others have done, too.

His parents, who constantly tried to suppress his natural aggression, usually took the side of his friends who tormented him. It wasn't that they liked them, on the contrary, they considered them bad and stupid children of bad and stupid parents. But Anton K. understood that his parents were instinctively on the side of the stronger.

Anton K.'s parents never failed to advise him that we should always look to find blame in ourselves. We have to blame ourselves first, and Anton K. understood that he should always look for other people's guilt in himself.

Anton K. developed the reflex of looking for guilt within himself. He would get angry and want to accuse other people, but his reaction was to take the guilt upon himself. To begin with, he accumulated piles, and then mountains of guilt. Then Anton K. did two things: first, he decided to consider himself bad; second, he became resentful toward the eternally innocent.

Once he had realized that he was bad, Anton K. felt his badness as a choking sensation in his throat, as an evil torture. He hadn't noticed anything similar among the people he knew. Despite this, he sensed there must be other people who experienced the same tormenting pain of their own badness. He had no way of knowing that there weren't many people like him, and that other people despised them. Some of them became saints by accident.

At the age of nine, Anton K. understood that the World was an unsure and confusing place. Whenever he came home after a beating, his parents would usually calm him down and express their sympathy, but then they wouldn't miss out on the chance to remark that the person who received the beating was also to blame for not defending himself.

Then they said he was to blame for standing up to the stronger child and not walking away.

This ambiguity confused Anton K. and he became more and more uncertain about what was right and what was wrong in the World. He didn't know whether he should stand up for himself or walk away. He began to have doubts about everything. The only certain thing was that none of this made him feel good.

At about the age of nine, Anton K. understood that people no longer treated him kindly as a child. His mother liked to say to her girlfriends, and made sure that Anton K. heard as well, "Up to the age of seven, the child is king, from seven to seventeen a slave, and after that a friend." His mother took particular delight in saying "from seven to seventeen a slave." Anton K. didn't want to be a slave. He hated the idea of slavery.

Again, when he was nine years old, Anton K. noted that like other people from other families, his mother never shed a tear for his suffering. She didn't shed a tear even when she was bad—to him or in general. She cried sometimes when she experienced physical pain. Most often when she believed someone had offended her. She sincerely and profoundly suffered when she considered herself hurt or offended. Once, when Anton K. had hurt himself quite badly, his mother was also in pain. She moaned and sobbed for so long that eventually he began to feel sorry for her and he forgot about his pain and started crying for hers.

Anton K.'s mother liked it when someone else cried for her. Anton K. understood that people as a rule liked someone else to cry for them. He also understood that people like crying for themselves, but not for someone else's pain.

Anton K. saw healthy people complaining to sick people, rich people complaining to poor people, and strong people looking for a tear of sympathy from the weak. Years later, Anton K. came across the following film title: *The Rich Also Cry.* He gave a muffled and spiteful laugh.

Anton K.'s mother also employed another tactic, which had a brilliant effect on his developing sense of guilt. Sometimes she would take to her bed and lie there all day long with her eyes shut like a biblical martyr reconciled to her agonies. Anton K. tiptoed helplessly around her and prayed to God, whom he hadn't yet heard about, to forgive him. Anton K. didn't yet know that women menstruated.

When his suffering mother got tired of making him tiptoe around her in silence, she would leap up and put all her energy into making noise by screaming with her unpleasant female voice, rattling pots and pans, and washing the floor with a pungent disinfectant, which made Anton K. slip and fall and then feel guilty for being clumsy.

One day Anton K. saw his mother crying inconsolably (he had already understood that people are capable of crying solely for themselves) at a funeral. It was the funeral of someone who had died suddenly, someone whom Anton K.'s mother had treated very badly until the day he died. Anton K. couldn't believe his eyes when he saw his mother sobbing. For a long time he thought about why she was crying. Only years later did he discover that people cry like that out of a superstitious fear of vengeance.

When he had grown to a height of about four feet and three inches above the surface of the Earth, Anton K. began to experience a serious interest in the details of his creation. He tried to ask some adults, but everyone he asked gave him unsatisfactory and vague answers. Anton K. was one of the new generation of children who couldn't be fooled with stories of storks, but the word sex was still taboo. For one of Anton's generation to say the word sex was tantamount to drawing a swastika on the school wall. So the children of Anton K.'s generation grew up in a state of exciting ignorance.

The most frequent answer Anton K. got was that he would understand everything about his creation when he grew up. His mother had told him when he was very little that he had been in her tummy and then came out. The thought that he had been in her tummy produced a certain feeling of repulsion in Anton K. He had once seen a squashed cat with its guts sticking out of its ripped tummy. The thought that he might have been somewhere like that was not pleasant.

Anton K. didn't know how much he would have to grow up in order to understand how he was created, but his suspicious mind made him assume there must be some answer he could get immediately. One day, when rummaging through the things in his parents' room, Anton K. found a book about family relations hidden among the underwear. It was full of shocking pictures of dissected bodies, which were almost incomprehensible, and for that reason exciting. There were a lot of naively drawn illustrations of sexual organs with arrows pointing to them. At the end of each arrow there was an incomprehensible word, as if someone had wanted to condemn each bad part of the human body.

From this rich gallery of frightening pictures, Anton K. more or less gained a vague understanding of the mystery of conception. It was called the sexual act, coitus, insemination, and other words. All these words brought about in Anton K. a sweet sensation of repulsion, similar to that which he had experienced when he had studied his own excrement. From what he had read, he understood that he had been created by means of a secret act described in the hidden books as *intimacy*. From that moment on, *intimacy* became another word for *dirty*.

Sometimes Anton K. would hear the adults talk about things he had read in the shameful book filled with cross-sections of male and female torsos. When they spoke about it, they grinned revoltingly or contorted their faces into meaningful expressions, or changed their voices. They would turn up their eyes, giggle, and lower their voices. They would say the word *sex* with a contorted face. They looked grotesque, but Anton K. didn't yet know what *grotesque* meant. Anton K. suddenly understood that one day when he grew up and tried all "this," he would then talk meaningfully about "that business" and he would laugh revoltingly. When he understood this, he experienced a sense of impatience for this day to come.

One day, when he was ten years old, Anton K. experienced an unfamiliar, burning, and insurmountable terror. The terror was caused by a sudden thought that pierced his mind and exploded. It was: One day . . . my parents will die and I will be all alone. Then later . . . later—Anton K. thought as he tossed and turned in his bed sheets, damp from perspiration—I will die too.

From that day on, there was no other thought in his head. His games with his cruel and stupid friends and studying his useless school subjects would take his mind off it for a moment. Then his mind, quivering with fear, would return to the thought of his death. And there was no way out.

It was during this time that one of Anton K.'s friends killed himself. Everyone was shocked. How, how is it possible? his parents sobbed. How is it possible, when life is only just starting, when all the possibilities of life are in front of you . . . Why, why? Everyone who knew the boy sobbed inconsolably. Anton K. didn't cry, because even though he was tormented by pain, he still was unable to pretend to cry for someone else's pain.

He didn't cry because an intense thought came to his mind. One of those thoughts that come suddenly and bear the stamp of Truth itself.

It was the following thought: the only salvation from the fear of death is to cause it yourself when you decide to. With this thought, Anton K. understood that sooner or later he would rid himself of his fear in this way.

Even before his tenth year, Anton K. experienced the strong desire to understand the difference between boys and girls. He didn't have any sisters. The girls at school were his natural enemies, like every boy. When his friends made him stand naked in front of the girls, he experienced terrifying shame. But he sensed, without understanding clearly, that in the future he would become passionate about showing his naked body.

He was not yet able to understand that many people want to show their naked bodies, and even more their naked souls, to other people. But the buttons that suffocate them cannot be undone from their buttonholes, and this is why people are forever clothed and stifled by their garments.

Anton K. had not seen a naked body of the other sex. There were no pornographic magazines at that time, and nudity was banned in all the Russian and Bulgarian films that were shown on television in the evening. Children were banned from watching television in the evening. However, Anton K. became aware on a daily basis of the almost imperceptibly developing differences between him and the girls.

Ten-year-old girls were all ugly anyway, or at least that's what Anton K. thought, but the strange differences interested him. He couldn't understand the long hair, the different smell of their bodies, why they squatted to pee (he had secretly watched the girls in the park). He was intrigued by girls' dresses and games. Girls seemed very peculiar and unnatural. Even the way they ran intrigued and annoyed him. He thought it strange that when girls ran they kicked their heels out to one side.

When Anton K. was ten he touched a girl for the first time without a feeling of unpleasantness. Of course, he had held hands with girls in kindergarten, but that was because he had to. Even then he had sensed the difference between girls and boys.

When he touched a girl for the first time without hitting her or pulling her hair, he experienced a huge sense of excitement. This is how it happened: One day when they were lining up in classes, he found himself standing in his row next to an amazingly beautiful young lady who didn't possess any of the annoying traits of the other girls. She was wonderful. She had bright-blue eyes, black hair, and such fine features that the sun seemed to send special, softer rays to shine on her. Anton K. had known this girl for almost six months but had never really thought about her. His mind was too preoccupied with things he had to understand.

Now the excitement at the beauty of the blue-eyed girl made him breathless. She was standing right next to him, observing him with a stolen but smiling gaze. The head teacher issued the order: "Line up at arms' length." Anton K. timidly stretched out his arm and placed it on her shoulder. This was the beginning of his first love.

Anton K. had experienced strong excitement before, but he

hadn't understood what it was. It was amazing but it wasn't any-thing unfamiliar. He had experienced a little joy and pain in his life, but mainly fear and shame. He had even experienced some-thing similar to love and desperation, and these are difficult feel-ings for a child. He had experienced love for his grandfather. He was the only person in the world with whom he could talk for hours on end. His grandfather's stories were wonderful, ancient, and nice. He smelled like an old radio in a wooden box. He had experienced desperation when his grandfather fell ill and soon after that died.

Anton K. had never before experienced the excitement he felt when he touched the blue-eyed girl. He felt a wave of nausea, his heart seemed to pump in his chest and throat, then flutter in his stomach, and pulsate in the very bottom of his body. But it wasn't unpleasant. Not in the least.

And so after a week of strange sensations of excitement, Anton K. realized that he was in love.

Anton K. began to do everything he could to be closer to the girl. She was very proud! She walked with raised shoulders and the elegant poise of her graceful head accentuating the neck muscles. She walked with the allure of a miniature ballerina trembling as she goes out onto the stage. Whenever she appeared, Anton K. would hide somewhere, behind the thistles, in the shadows of the apartment blocks, among the shrubbery left over from the time when the district was a village of single-story houses. The girl with the black hair and blue eyes would sometimes walk past him at a distance of no more than a few feet, while Anton K. would be sitting hidden behind a tree quivering. He understood that hiding and shyly observing things he liked would become one of his essential traits. Anton K. realized that he was some-thing like a spy or thief and felt happy and excited.

He would secretly crawl behind old, derelict fences and look at the light footsteps of the blue-eyed girl through the gaps. In each gap he could see her face, her neck, her hands, her hair, her eyes, and would steal them for himself, to fill his lonely, hidden dreams with their images. Sometimes the direct effect of the girl's image was so strong that Anton K. would feel sick. He would get dizzy, his legs would tremble, and all he wanted at these moments was to be as far away from her as possible, so that he could dream about them alone. But he couldn't stop himself secretly following her.

They took the same route to school in the morning. He would walk unevenly, speeding up then slowing down again, hoping to see her—first her black hair, then her slender body, then all of her. He knew her school timetable off by heart, and he would sneak out of school early in the afternoon or stay behind to wait for her to appear. When she appeared, Anton K. would be overcome by a canine excitement, hurrying up, bending over, and walking awkwardly.

After a long period of observing her shyly from various hiding places, Anton K. understood that he wanted the girl to notice him. Then, when she started noticing him, he would do everything possible to make her like him. He had no idea how to do this.

He wanted to be tall and handsome, but he was short for his age, and he still had a very childish, plump face. He felt envious of the other boys whom the girls liked. He had heard the girls at his school say that they liked older and taller boys. Anton K. knew boys like that and he hated them. They already had fluff on their upper lips. They were slim and sinewy, with nice, shiny tracksuits or expensive, tight jeans. Most of all, the girls liked boys with long, fair hair, or those whose parents lived abroad and who got a lot of pocket money from their grandparents. Anton K. understood that he possessed nothing that girls liked.

Somehow, perhaps because of his already highly developed sense of failure, Anton K. realized from the very outset that he wasn't going to be noticed. He experienced all the torment of indifference, but he couldn't stop. Like someone sliding down an icy slope and refusing to hold on to anything, Anton K. continued to make attempts to be noticed. Each one more ridiculous and clumsy than the last. When he saw the girl, he would throw his backpack high into the air and catch it awkwardly, or he would put on a low masculine voice and shout something to his friends, or he would comb back his hair with his fingers.

He would even walk hunched over like a cowboy and laugh too loudly. He hoped that with such inept behaviour he would attract her attention. He wanted the girl to think that he was a hooligan, a real lion, an underage delinquent. The girl would sometimes cast a fleeting, heavenly glance in his direction, stealing his heart and then abandoning him again. Anton K. began to live for these momentary glances. Nothing else interested him. He had not yet understood that most people live only for a handful of moments in their lives. He did not yet know that many people had already experienced these moments and that all that remained in their lives was what happened between their three daily meals.

When he was twelve, Anton K. was tired of admiring the blue-eyed, inaccessible girl. He even sensed a slight feeling of malicious joy that he didn't love her like he used to. He understood that when a feeling is not reciprocated for a long time, it turns into displeasure, and then into indifference. He understood that the same thing happens to beautiful, new feelings as happens to the best Christmas presents. They may be pure, bright, and exciting, but over time they grow old, lose their color and fragrance, they crack, and one day they get cast into the cold cellar of the soul.

At the age of thirteen, Anton K. had already experienced his first sexual thrills. He had fondled two or three early-developing girls. He had succeeded in awkwardly squeezing their breasts and kissing them clumsily on their necks. They hadn't offered any resistance (except when he tried to feel them a bit lower down, then the girls' hands would stop him). These sweaty pleasures disgusted him. He thought them reptilian and undignified. Then he would think back to the proud girl with the blue eyes. Compared to the mousy-haired, disproportionally pubescent creatures whose underdeveloped breasts he had squeezed, the blue-eyed girl seemed as inaccessible and pure as a diamond.

Anton K. understood that he would spend the rest of his life panting wretchedly while he touched and kissed these soft, smelly, sweaty, and slimy creatures. While all the time dreaming of touching a beautiful diamond.

Until the age of sixteen, Anton K. spent his time diligently studying all the bad habits that in his opinion made adults differ-ent from children. He wanted to become an adult as quickly as possible, because he thought that would help him turn his back on all the humiliations he had experienced in his childhood.

He was by nature shy and he learned to smoke to hide the clumsiness of his gestures behind his cigarette. He smoked to overcome his excitement every time he made a new acquain-tance. He smoked in order to mask his inability to hold an interesting conversation.

He smoked in order to conceal how plump and childlike his face still was. Without the assistance of a cigarette he would writhe in embarrassment and wonder how to control his disobe-dient hands and where to direct his embarrassed gaze. Anton K. understood how cunning adults can be. You take out a cigarette and say casually, "Have you got a light?" You inhale smoke, you feel a bit dizzy, you cough, and then you start talking about how you want to give up smoking and you feel calm and good. When there's an awkward pause, you light another cigarette.

At about the age of sixteen, and with the greatest of satisfac-tion, Anton K. discovered the effect of alcohol. He was by now at high school and his school friends were not as stupid or evil as those in his local primary school. This is what happened: One day a dozen or so of his closest school friends decided to get together and do something. There was no particular occasion, it was just a fine May afternoon. They got together in the apart-ment of one of the boys who was clearly more experienced than the others in the important matters of life. To begin with they felt a bit embarrassed in the apartment and stood like statues. It was the first time they had organized something as sponta-neous as this, and they didn't really know what to do. It wasn't anybody's birthday and there weren't any presents to give, or any good wishes to offer. After a few awkward minutes they sat down and began gradually to relax. They wanted to behave as if they were real adults. They wanted to be casual and free of all their childhood anxieties. But they were anxious. Then the host suggested they have a drink. They all looked at one another and agreed like co-conspirators rebelling against the prohibitions of adults. The boys and the girls. It was at that moment that Anton K. understood that they were girls who in the future would become his friends and that they weren't arrogant and different, but sociable and friendly.

That evening Anton K. drank a lot of his friend's father's cognac. The host claimed that his father was very liberal and talked to him about his lovers. The apartment was big, clearly very expensive, but empty. The liberal father and the unknown mother were conveniently working abroad. They all drank his father's cognac, whiskey, and liqueur, in fact everything they could find in the liberal father's liquor cabinet. Anton K. for the first time experienced envy. He understood that only rich fathers can afford to be liberal and have so many expensive drinks in their expensive homes. Then he felt dizzy and joyful. He began laughing and finally realized that he was collapsing and falling asleep.

When he woke up, he found himself in the arms of one of the girls. Her head was resting on his shoulder and she was snoring quietly. Anton K. remained lying there, he was still dizzy, but happy, despite a terrible headache. Through the fog of his brain he understood that alcohol made people uninhibited and interesting, and so nice that if they had one iota of brain cells, they would drink all the time. He thought this and kissed the girl on the forehead, on the cheek, on the lips, and then fell asleep again.

When he woke up a few hours later, he was overcome by a sense of guilt. He felt nauseous and anxious. He sensed he had done something wrong.

It was the first time he hadn't been home all night. He hadn't gone to school. He was alone and still drunk. He understood that alcohol is quite pleasant in the evening. The mornings after are dreadful. The girl had gone, and the sun was shining brightly and pointlessly in the empty and untidy room.

Anton K. quietly crept out of the flat. He walked for about half an hour through the bright morning streets. Then, feeling depressed, he understood that one of the things he would come to hate most in his life was walking through the streets vulnerable and naked under the pointless, bright morning light of the sun, alone, guilty, and half-drunk. He understood that this would inevitably happen to him as a consequence of the joy-filled nights before the mornings after. The price he would have to pay for his pleasant evenings would be getting hauled before crowds of judges and executioners. Before people hurrying to work and staring disapprovingly into his intoxicated face.

At the age of nineteen, Anton K. was called up to do his national service in the army. He tried to grow into a man, but it was a torturous process. Anton K. suffered like a child when the umbilical cord was roughly ripped away from the entire world he had known until now. It wasn't so much the physical suffering that pained him. The cold, fatigue, and excruciating physical exercises helped him to a certain extent to ignore the humiliations and spiritual pain which they brought about. He understood the meaning of real, systematic humiliation for absurd reasons. Anton K. also understood that the junior sergeants, officers, and older soldiers were not humiliating him and his comrades out of malice.

They were being humiliated because the abstract State required it. The abstract State had entrusted them with the task of crushing the dignity of the younger, helpless boys, to turn them into acquiescent, obedient, complacent, and patient man-machines. Anton K. thought about the obedient, frowning, cigarette-smoking men like robots going complacently every morning to their humiliating work and understood that this is what was meant by becoming a man. At that moment Anton K. also understood that the State was his personal enemy and started to despise it.

One day in his twentieth year, Anton K. committed a petty misdemeanor.

It was a hot day and he hadn't buttoned up his greatcoat properly during parade. A senior officer happened to be taking the parade that day. He summoned Anton K., who tried to button it up quickly, but he realized that it was a foolish thing to do and he dragged his feet and his non-regulation greatcoat over to the parade officer. The officer stared at Anton K. as he mumbled his report, then he screamed at him. Anton K. was so scared that he almost shat his pants. He felt almost the same way as when his mother had discovered his secret piles of excrement. He experienced the real, servile fear of a grown man. It was the fear of the brutal and indifferent cruelty that superior men manifest toward their inferiors.

As was expected, Anton K. was given a terrifyingly cruel punishment. It consisted of every day for sixteen hours wearing a gas mask, running with a gas mask, marching with a gas mask, crawling with a gas mask, leaping over trenches and barbed wire with a gas mask, and even reading the regulations with his gas mask on. Anton. K. had to spend fifteen days wearing his gas mask. It was given the absurd name of "retraining." Anton K. thought bitterly that he was clearly not ready to become a man and needed to be retrained.

During his punishment Anton K. was scared of dying for the first time in his life, not in the abstract sense like when he was a child, but in an entirely real, specific, and miserable way. He didn't want to die, and he felt that running twelve miles every day with the ugly and suffocating gas mask on his face in the terrible afternoon heat would certainly kill him. He lost twenty-two pounds. Half of his comrades who were undergoing the same punishment collapsed with exhaustion and had to be taken to the hospital.

Anton K. understood that he was ashamed. He just didn't have the strength to collapse and give up, or feign exhaustion and thus be saved. He still had a little strength left and he was ashamed to give in. So he carried on. He ran, he crawled, he marched, he suffocated—sixteen hours every day. He understood that when stimulated by shame and stubborn and acquiescent obedience human strength knows no bounds. He also understood that such stupid things as pride and honor are human inventions created to confuse the minds of idiots.

It didn't kill him, and he should have been proud that he was so tough and resilient! Anton K. understood that this was ridiculous and absurd and that he would never accept it.

From that moment on he thought of everybody who proudly

considered themselves to be tough and resilient as utter fools. He decided that he would betray every cause in his life, if it began to torment him or endanger his life for its sake.

During those frightening days, Anton K. discovered two enormous things he hadn't known before—real friendship and God. In his uneventful school life protected by relatively humane rules, he had never experienced a particular need for the support of a friend. His high-school friends had been no more than interesting boys with whom he liked to talk about the meaning of life and girls. They had never helped each other in the true meaning of the word, there had been no need. But it had been reassuring to discover that they all experienced the same fears and doubts. The revelations made at the age of eighteen saved them from the hidden torments they experienced when they were fifteen. This was indeed very reassuring.

However, as he endured his punishment, Anton K. felt the real need for somebody to give him a strong shoulder to lean on, and the courage and kindness to support him. Or perhaps, save him.

He found such a friend. He was a tall, thin boy who at first glance looked completely helpless. However, Anton K. sensed when he looked into his pure blue eyes that there was something incredibly powerful which protected the soul and body of this boy from the pains of the outside world and internal torment, as strong as the impenetrable armor of a tank. The boy radiated a sense of bright tranquillity. Anton K. quickly became friends with him. The boy was so good-natured that he immediately accepted the friendship of the tormented and frightened Anton K. He didn't scrutinize him, nor did he treat him diffidently as so many young men do during the period of their transformation into men. One day they just sat down opposite each other on the verge of collapsing from fatigue: Anton K., frightened by the savage cruelty of life, the boy smiling calmly and positively at something which only he could see as he gazed into the sky. They sat next to each other and became friends. From that day on, merely the proximity of the boy was sufficient for Anton K. to feel stronger and more confident. He felt calm and sensed that whatever they did to him, he would endure while his friend was close to him. However, Anton K. could not understand where his friend's strength and confidence came from and how it was transmitted to him like benign radiation. Then he understood. The boy believed in God. He believed so generously, purely, and deeply that even when he spoke about something trivial, it was like a quiet and beautiful eulogy to God. Anton K. understood from his friend that God existed, and that inspired him. He began zealously to believe, and his heart melted with excitement. He also understood that there was Hope and he began passionately to hope.

Anton K. continued to believe and to hope, but many years would have to pass before he began to understand that Hope was pain, in the same way that God who had given his Son in redemption for all the anger and insanity of people with his wounds was also pain. Anton K. understood that God was love, and that love causes pain. Anton K. was unable to love God calmly and generously like his friend. Anton K. loved God jealously and painfully. Years after his restorative punishment, Anton K. was to understand that he always turned to God when he was frightened and desperate, that he would turn to God not with a smile but with tears.

After leaving the army, Anton K. never again saw his friend who had enlightened him with Belief and given him Hope. He somehow didn't want to see him again. After they had completed their punishment, whenever Anton K. saw his friend in the barracks, he would experience a strange but painful sense of excitement. Anton K.'s enormous capacity for guilt made him feel like a tainted criminal bound for Hell, unlike his angelically pure friend. The clear and kind eyes of his friend made Anton K.'s evil heart writhe in torment and guilt for its thoughts and deeds before God.

Years passed and Anton K. somehow managed to graduate from college. The years in the army had turned him into a slender and muscular young man. His face had become transformed from its previously childish features into something pleasant to behold. His slender body, pleasant face, perspicacity and wit (developed over the years as a defensive bastion against the hostile outside world) made him a favorite with women.

Anton K. wasn't very academic, he wasn't very sporty, he didn't like traveling or romance, unlike most of his college friends. He wasn't very successful with women either. He liked attracting them and making them like him and even fall in love with him, while he enjoyed his indifference toward them. Anton K. wanted to get his own back on his mother and on the blue-eyed girl with the tender face. He wanted to get his own back on the people who had humiliated him and take revenge for the boundless guilt he carried with him. He didn't feel guilty for the women who cried for him, humiliated themselves for his sake, or lost their minds for his sake. His feeling of guilt had become encapsulated like a tuberculous cavern within the years of accumulated anger, humiliation, and bitterness. What was left of his soul was light, frivolous, and empty. Nobody else was aware of this cavern and they considered him carefree and amusing. Occasionally the cavern would fissure and suppurate with a bloody seepage of guilt. Anton K. understood that this bloody guilt was guilt before God, whom he recalled only when he was unhappy. Whenever the blood of guilt seeped from the cavern, Anton K. would get drunk and the cavern would close.

When he graduated from college, Anton K. understood that he needed to find a job. He was enticed by the thought of working and earning enough money to become relatively independent. At the same time, one of the women on whom Anton K. was taking his revenge, but liked more than the others, got pregnant, and Anton K. decided that his life, filled as it was with doubts, suspicions, pointless discoveries of new, unnecessary truths, had to be given some meaning. He still couldn't understand that, unless he made the required effort, the birth of a child would not give meaning to his life.

The child was born. Anton K. couldn't understand whether he was happy or just experiencing a profound sense of fear of his future responsibilities. He trembled as he clumsily and fearfully held the little red baby and felt a strange sense of embarrassment in front of his relatives. He then understood that at the most important moments in life, he was unable to be happy, dance, sing songs of joy, cry, or experience those moments like people were supposed to. He could only stand there with his arms by his sides, dazed and confused.

Over time Anton K. learned to love his little daughter. He loved her when he was doing good things for her and her mother. When he was being bad—for example, when he was unable to earn enough money or be kind and forgiving or take on the responsibility of being a good father and husband—he became painfully cold toward his wife and daughter. Once again he felt overcome and suffocated by the sickness of guilt. As an inexperienced young man unaccustomed to serious responsibilities, Anton K. did not do a particularly good job. He often treated his family coldly and that tormented him. He wanted to be good, but he couldn't. He tried hard but was exhausted by the demands of life. He began to understand that he was becoming frustrated and old, and slowly losing all semblance of his human image. He rarely allowed himself to relax. And when he did, the occasions were banal, dry, and boring. On very rare occasions, he would leave his wife at home and go out with his friends, to drink beer, engage in unnecessary conversations, and then come home in a state of foolish high spirits. At first, his wife didn't seem to mind. However, as life began to exhaust her, she began to treat Anton K. more and more coldly, after every evening of relaxation.

Anton K. didn't earn enough money. He spent unwisely and didn't pay enough attention to detail. Only years later would he understand that in marriage it's the details that are the most important. He became introverted and would trip over his wife's shoes, which drove him crazy. Only years later would Anton K. understand that relaxation is not possible within marriage. He understood that once you have taken the rough, cheerless road toward middle age, you have no right to even a moment of relaxation. It just takes a second's lack of attention and life can crush you like a car, run you over and throw you into some empty gutter.

However, he realized this only after he split up with his wife.

Anton K. left his wife for another woman. Living a boring,

tedious family life had brought him to understand that the accumulation of material wealth could bring a certain degree of satisfaction. However, Anton K. lived at a time when young graduates like himself received pitifully low salaries, and he painfully and subconsciously began to look for something that might make him a little happier. His growing daughter gave him joy, but Anton K. understood that such joys were slightly hypocritical, in that people had simply decided, as if by some law of nature incomprehensible to Anton K., that children should bring joy to their parents. Anton K. clearly understood that if he was rich, if he was good at his job, if he had more self-esteem, life might be happier and more pleasant.

He imagined sunny holidays in beautiful places with his happy, contented family, and without the miserable and humiliating need to save money. He imagined opulent and abundant shopping trips. He had discovered that almost all so-called "happy families" went on such trips to enhance and enrich their level of material satisfaction. He had understood that happy families are those who lived calmly and affluently. He recalled the liberal father of his school friend and experienced a sense of anger and envy toward everyone who had enough money to be content and liberal and well-protected from the harsh blows of life. He had seen that such people accept their illnesses and the loss of those close to them with a sort of self-satisfied tranquility. They were more preoccupied with expensive medicines from abroad and expensive coffins than suffering and desperation. He thought it was a stupid lie to say that a good and happy life could only be found in a poor family. He hadn't seen any evidence of that. Tormented by his poverty, which was more humiliating than it was terrible, he looked for salvation outside his family. Far from the quiet, increasingly dissatisfied, and almost spiteful gaze of his wife.

Anton K. met a woman he liked. She was clever, pretty, blunt, relatively rich, one of those women who, in contrast to him, was never short of money. Anton K. had long since learned not to be embarrassed when women paid the bills as recompense for his wit and body. He liked the fact that she was so emancipated that any man would have been envious of him. Her apartment was bigger than Anton's, completely empty, and entirely her own. She had her own bank account and no annoying family in Sofia. Her fridge was always full of alcohol and delicious things. Anton K. became more and more attached to her. He began to come home late, and then for two or three days he didn't go home at all. He lied shamelessly to his wife, saying that he had to work late, travel outside the city, and so on. Anton K. understood what it was to be unfaithful—how ugly, pleasant, detestable, and exciting it was. His guilt sickness became so acute that Anton K. began to show physical symptoms of illness. It affected his heart, and he began to experience sudden panic attacks. Then he understood that if you live in a web of lies concealing a painful secret, it won't be long before you die. He told his wife everything. Soon after that they split up.

Anton K. went to live with his new woman, only they didn't get married. He waited, made excuses, and avoided making promises. He understood that if he was to live with this new woman in the same way as he lived with his old wife—and to make matters worse, she was rich and he was poor—the relationship would go the same miserable way as his first one. Anton K.'s life became confused and uncertain. There was nothing firm to grasp on to. That didn't scare him, apart from in the mornings when he woke up bathed in sweat after dreams of a menacing future. He understood that life would go mercilessly on, drawing closer to old age, filled with deceit and fear, confusing and completely incomprehensible.

The years passed, and Anton K. began to understand more and more new things. He understood that women are completely different from men. Then he understood that there was almost no difference, and then he understood that neither the one nor the other was true. The years passed and Anton K. sensed the fear of growing old, he experienced the banal pleasures of depravity, paid the bitter price for his independence, learned the intoxicating allure of money, and ate from the shameful spoon of poverty.

The years passed, and Anton K. understood what it was to be healthy and strong, when for the first time he realized what it was to be ill and feeble, and he understood the crushing weight of loneliness. He discovered the joy of good, hard work, he discovered the humiliation of slavery, and he discovered the exhaustion of inactivity. He understood how repulsive it is to be a normal and ordinary man, but how terrifying it is to be mad and misunderstood.

The years passed, and one day in an indifferent year, just like the previous ones, the number of which merely annoyed Anton K., he woke up feeling terribly tired. He lay in bed for hours. When he got up, he realized that something in him had changed. He sluggishly dragged his tired legs into the bathroom. His arms, chest, face, and mind were overcome with fatigue. He looked at himself in the mirror. With a feeling of sad pity for himself, he realized that he was old. He understood that he had discovered this at least four years too late. He understood that the future would no longer offer him any interesting things to understand. He went back to bed. How had it come to this? Anton K. did not understand. And he didn't want to understand. And without understanding why, he knew that he would no longer want to understand anything. He was far too tired of understanding things.

KALIN TERZIYSKI was born in 1970 in Sofia, Bulgaria. He earned a doctorate in medicine and practiced psychiatry for several years before becoming a writer. He is the author of several collections of stories and two novels.

DAVID MOSSOP translates from Bulgarian, Russian, and French. He received his BA at the University of Bristol, has an MA in Linguistics, and a PhD in Linguistisc and Semantics. He teaches translation at the New Bulgarian University.

MICHAL AJVAZ, *The Golden Age.*
The Other City.

PIERRE ALBERT-BIROT, *Grabinoulor.*

YUZ ALESHKOVSKY, *Kangaroo.*

FELIPE ALFAU, *Chromos.*
Locos.

JOE AMATO, *Samuel Taylor's Last Night.*

IVAN ÂNGELO, *The Celebration.*
The Tower of Glass.

ANTÓNIO LOBO ANTUNES, *Knowledge of Hell.*
The Splendor of Portugal.

ALAIN ARIAS-MISSON, *Theatre of Incest.*

JOHN ASHBERY & JAMES SCHUYLER, *A Nest of Ninnies.*

ROBERT ASHLEY, *Perfect Lives.*

GABRIELA AVIGUR-ROTEM, *Heatwave and Crazy Birds.*

DJUNA BARNES, *Ladies Almanack.*
Ryder.

JOHN BARTH, *Letters.*
Sabbatical.

DONALD BARTHELME, *The King.*
Paradise.

SVETISLAV BASARA, *Chinese Letter.*

MIQUEL BAUÇÀ, *The Siege in the Room.*

RENÉ BELLETTO, *Dying.*

MAREK BIENCZYK, *Transparency.*

ANDREI BITOV, *Pushkin House.*

ANDREJ BLATNIK, *You Do Understand.*
Law of Desire.

LOUIS PAUL BOON, *Chapel Road.*
My Little War.
Summer in Termuren.

ROGER BOYLAN, *Killoyle.*

IGNÁCIO DE LOYOLA BRANDÃO, *Anonymous Celebrity.*
Zero.

BONNIE BREMSER, *Troia: Mexican Memoirs.*

CHRISTINE BROOKE-ROSE, *Amalgamemnon.*

BRIGID BROPHY, *In Transit.*
The Prancing Novelist.

GERALD L. BRUNS, *Modern Poetry and the Idea of Language.*

GABRIELLE BURTON, *Heartbreak Hotel.*

MICHEL BUTOR, *Degrees.*
Mobile.

G. CABRERA INFANTE, *Infante's Inferno.*
Three Trapped Tigers.

JULIETA CAMPOS, *The Fear of Losing Eurydice.*

ANNE CARSON, *Eros the Bittersweet.*

ORLY CASTEL-BLOOM, *Dolly City.*

LOUIS-FERDINAND CÉLINE, *North.*
Conversations with Professor Y.
London Bridge.

MARIE CHAIX, *The Laurels of Lake Constance.*

HUGO CHARTERIS, *The Tide Is Right.*

ERIC CHEVILLARD, *Demolishing Nisard.*
The Author and Me.

MARC CHOLODENKO, *Mordechai Schamz.*

JOSHUA COHEN, *Witz.*

EMILY HOLMES COLEMAN, *The Shutter of Snow.*

ERIC CHEVILLARD, *The Author and Me.*

ROBERT COOVER, *A Night at the Movies.*

STANLEY CRAWFORD, *Log of the S.S.*
The Mrs Unguentine.
Some Instructions to My Wife.

RENÉ CREVEL, *Putting My Foot in It.*

RALPH CUSACK, *Cadenza.*

NICHOLAS DELBANCO, *Sherbrookes.*
The Count of Concord.

NIGEL DENNIS, *Cards of Identity.*

PETER DIMOCK, *A Short Rhetoric for Leaving the Family.*

ARIEL DORFMAN, *Konfidenz.*

COLEMAN DOWELL, *Island People.*
Too Much Flesh and Jabez.

ARKADII DRAGOMOSHCHENKO, *Dust.*

RIKKI DUCORNET, *Phosphor in Dreamland.*
The Complete Butcher's Tales.

RIKKI DUCORNET (cont.), *The Jade Cabinet*.
The Fountains of Neptune.

WILLIAM EASTLAKE, *The Bamboo Bed*.
Castle Keep.
Lyric of the Circle Heart.

JEAN ECHENOZ, *Chopin's Move*.

STANLEY ELKIN, *A Bad Man*.
Criers and Kibitzers, Kibitzers and Criers.
The Dick Gibson Show.
The Franchiser.
The Living End.
Mrs. Ted Bliss.

FRANÇOIS EMMANUEL, *Invitation to a Voyage*.

PAUL EMOND, *The Dance of a Sham*.

SALVADOR ESPRIU, *Ariadne in the Grotesque Labyrinth*.

LESLIE A. FIEDLER, *Love and Death in the American Novel*.

JUAN FILLOY, *Op Oloop*.

ANDY FITCH, *Pop Poetics*.

GUSTAVE FLAUBERT, *Bouvard and Pécuchet*.

KASS FLEISHER, *Talking out of School*.

JON FOSSE, *Aliss at the Fire*.
Melancholy.

FORD MADOX FORD, *The March of Literature*.

MAX FRISCH, *I'm Not Stiller*.
Man in the Holocene.

CARLOS FUENTES, *Christopher Unborn*.
Distant Relations.
Terra Nostra.
Where the Air Is Clear.

TAKEHIKO FUKUNAGA, *Flowers of Grass*.

WILLIAM GADDIS, JR., *The Recognitions*.

JANICE GALLOWAY, *Foreign Parts*.
The Trick Is to Keep Breathing.

WILLIAM H. GASS, *Life Sentences*.
The Tunnel.
The World Within the Word.
Willie Masters' Lonesome Wife.

GÉRARD GAVARRY, *Hoppla! 1 2 3*.

ETIENNE GILSON, *The Arts of the Beautiful*.
Forms and Substances in the Arts.

C. S. GISCOMBE, *Giscome Road*.
Here.

DOUGLAS GLOVER, *Bad News of the Heart*.

WITOLD GOMBROWICZ, *A Kind of Testament*.

PAULO EMÍLIO SALES GOMES, *P's Three Women*.

GEORGI GOSPODINOV, *Natural Novel*.

JUAN GOYTISOLO, *Count Julian*.
Juan the Landless.
Makbara.
Marks of Identity.

HENRY GREEN, *Blindness*.
Concluding.
Doting.
Nothing.

JACK GREEN, *Fire the Bastards!*

JIŘÍ GRUŠA, *The Questionnaire*.

MELA HARTWIG, *Am I a Redundant Human Being?*

JOHN HAWKES, *The Passion Artist*.
Whistlejacket.

ELIZABETH HEIGHWAY, ED., *Contemporary Georgian Fiction*.

AIDAN HIGGINS, *Balcony of Europe*.
Blind Man's Bluff.
Bornholm Night-Ferry.
Langrishe, Go Down.
Scenes from a Receding Past.

KEIZO HINO, *Isle of Dreams*.

KAZUSHI HOSAKA, *Plainsong*.

ALDOUS HUXLEY, *Antic Hay*.
Point Counter Point.
Those Barren Leaves.
Time Must Have a Stop.

NAOYUKI II, *The Shadow of a Blue Cat*.

DRAGO JANČAR, *The Tree with No Name*.

MIKHEIL JAVAKHISHVILI, *Kvachi*.

GERT JONKE, *The Distant Sound*.
Homage to Czerny.
The System of Vienna.

FOR A FULL LIST OF PUBLICATIONS, VISIT: www.dalkeyarchive.com

JACQUES JOUET, *Mountain R.*
Savage.
Upstaged.
MIEKO KANAI, *The Word Book.*
YORAM KANIUK, *Life on Sandpaper.*
ZURAB KARUMIDZE, *Dagny.*
JOHN KELLY, *From Out of the City.*
HUGH KENNER, *Flaubert, Joyce and Beckett: The Stoic Comedians.*
Joyce's Voices.
DANILO KIŠ, *The Attic.*
The Lute and the Scars.
Psalm 44.
A Tomb for Boris Davidovich.
ANITA KONKKA, *A Fool's Paradise.*
GEORGE KONRÁD, *The City Builder.*
TADEUSZ KONWICKI, *A Minor Apocalypse.*
The Polish Complex.
ANNA KORDZAIA-SAMADASHVILI, *Me, Margarita.*
MENIS KOUMANDAREAS, *Koula.*
ELAINE KRAF, *The Princess of 72nd Street.*
JIM KRUSOE, *Iceland.*
AYSE KULIN, *Farewell: A Mansion in Occupied Istanbul.*
EMILIO LASCANO TEGUI, *On Elegance While Sleeping.*
ERIC LAURRENT, *Do Not Touch.*
VIOLETTE LEDUC, *La Bâtarde.*
EDOUARD LEVÉ, *Autoportrait.*
Newspaper.
Suicide.
Works.
MARIO LEVI, *Istanbul Was a Fairy Tale.*
DEBORAH LEVY, *Billy and Girl.*
JOSÉ LEZAMA LIMA, *Paradiso.*
ROSA LIKSOM, *Dark Paradise.*
OSMAN LINS, *Avalovara.*
The Queen of the Prisons of Greece.
FLORIAN LIPUŠ, *The Errors of Young Tjaž.*
GORDON LISH, *Peru.*
ALF MACLOCHLAINN, *Out of Focus.*
Past Habitual.

The Corpus in the Library.
RON LOEWINSOHN, *Magnetic Field(s).*
YURI LOTMAN, *Non-Memoirs.*
D. KEITH MANO, *Take Five.*
MINA LOY, *Stories and Essays of Mina Loy.*
MICHELINE AHARONIAN MARCOM, *A Brief History of Yes.*
The Mirror in the Well.
BEN MARCUS, *The Age of Wire and String.*
WALLACE MARKFIELD, *Teitlebaum's Window.*
DAVID MARKSON, *Reader's Block.*
Wittgenstein's Mistress.
CAROLE MASO, *AVA.*
HISAKI MATSUURA, *Triangle.*
LADISLAV MATEJKA & KRYSTYNA POMORSKA, EDS., *Readings in Russian Poetics: Formalist & Structuralist Views.*
HARRY MATHEWS, *Cigarettes.*
The Conversions.
The Human Country.
The Journalist.
My Life in CIA.
Singular Pleasures.
The Sinking of the Odradek.
Stadium.
Tlooth.
HISAKI MATSUURA, *Triangle.*
DONAL MCLAUGHLIN, *beheading the virgin mary, and other stories.*
JOSEPH MCELROY, *Night Soul and Other Stories.*
ABDELWAHAB MEDDEB, *Talismano.*
GERHARD MEIER, *Isle of the Dead.*
HERMAN MELVILLE, *The Confidence-Man.*
AMANDA MICHALOPOULOU, *I'd Like.*
STEVEN MILLHAUSER, *The Barnum Museum.*
In the Penny Arcade.
RALPH J. MILLS, JR., *Essays on Poetry.*
MOMUS, *The Book of Jokes.*
CHRISTINE MONTALBETTI, *The Origin of Man.*
Western.

NICHOLAS MOSLEY, *Accident.*
Assassins.
Catastrophe Practice.
A Garden of Trees.
Hopeful Monsters.
Imago Bird.
Inventing God.
Look at the Dark.
Metamorphosis.
Natalie Natalia.
Serpent.
WARREN MOTTE, *Fables of the Novel:*
French Fiction since 1990.
Fiction Now: The French Novel in the
21st Century.
Mirror Gazing.
Oulipo: A Primer of Potential Literature.
GERALD MURNANE, *Barley Patch.*
Inland.
YVES NAVARRE, *Our Share of Time.*
Sweet Tooth.
DOROTHY NELSON, *In Night's City.*
Tar and Feathers.
ESHKOL NEVO, *Homesick.*
WILFRIDO D. NOLLEDO, *But for*
the Lovers.
BORIS A. NOVAK, *The Master of*
Insomnia.
FLANN O'BRIEN, *At Swim-Two-Birds.*
The Best of Myles.
The Dalkey Archive.
The Hard Life.
The Poor Mouth.
The Third Policeman.
CLAUDE OLLIER, *The Mise-en-Scène.*
Wert and the Life Without End.
PATRIK OUŘEDNÍK, *Europeana.*
The Opportune Moment, 1855.
BORIS PAHOR, *Necropolis.*
FERNANDO DEL PASO, *News from*
the Empire.
Palinuro of Mexico.
ROBERT PINGET, *The Inquisitory.*
Mahu or The Material.
Trio.
MANUEL PUIG, *Betrayed by Rita*
Hayworth.

The Buenos Aires Affair.
Heartbreak Tango.
RAYMOND QUENEAU, *The Last Days.*
Odile.
Pierrot Mon Ami.
Saint Glinglin.
ANN QUIN, *Berg.*
Passages.
Three.
Tripticks.
ISHMAEL REED, *The Free-Lance*
Pallbearers.
The Last Days of Louisiana Red.
Ishmael Reed: The Plays.
Juice!
The Terrible Threes.
The Terrible Twos.
Yellow Back Radio Broke-Down.
JASIA REICHARDT, *15 Journeys Warsaw*
to London.
JOÃO UBALDO RIBEIRO, *House of the*
Fortunate Buddhas.
JEAN RICARDOU, *Place Names.*
RAINER MARIA RILKE,
The Notebooks of Malte Laurids Brigge.
JULIÁN RÍOS, *The House of Ulysses.*
Larva: A Midsummer Night's Babel.
Poundemonium.
ALAIN ROBBE-GRILLET, *Project for a*
Revolution in New York.
A Sentimental Novel.
AUGUSTO ROA BASTOS, *I the Supreme.*
DANIËL ROBBERECHTS, *Arriving in*
Avignon.
JEAN ROLIN, *The Explosion of the*
Radiator Hose.
OLIVIER ROLIN, *Hotel Crystal.*
ALIX CLEO ROUBAUD, *Alix's Journal.*
JACQUES ROUBAUD, *The Form of*
a City Changes Faster, Alas, Than the
Human Heart.
The Great Fire of London.
Hortense in Exile.
Hortense Is Abducted.
Mathematics: The Plurality of Worlds of
Lewis.
Some Thing Black.

RAYMOND ROUSSEL, *Impressions of Africa.*

VEDRANA RUDAN, *Night.*

PABLO M. RUIZ, *Four Cold Chapters on the Possibility of Literature.*

GERMAN SADULAEV, *The Maya Pill.*

TOMAŽ ŠALAMUN, *Soy Realidad.*

LYDIE SALVAYRE, *The Company of Ghosts.*
The Lecture.
The Power of Flies.

LUIS RAFAEL SÁNCHEZ, *Macho Camacho's Beat.*

SEVERO SARDUY, *Cobra & Maitreya.*

NATHALIE SARRAUTE, *Do You Hear Them?*
Martereau.
The Planetarium.

STIG SÆTERBAKKEN, *Siamese.*
Self-Control.
Through the Night.

ARNO SCHMIDT, *Collected Novellas.*
Collected Stories.
Nobodaddy's Children.
Two Novels.

ASAF SCHURR, *Motti.*

GAIL SCOTT, *My Paris.*

DAMION SEARLS, *What We Were Doing and Where We Were Going.*

JUNE AKERS SEESE, *Is This What Other Women Feel Too?*

BERNARD SHARE, *Inish.*
Transit.

VIKTOR SHKLOVSKY, *Bowstring.*
Literature and Cinematography.
Theory of Prose.
Third Factory.
Zoo, or Letters Not about Love.

PIERRE SINIAC, *The Collaborators.*

KJERSTI A. SKOMSVOLD, *The Faster I Walk, the Smaller I Am.*

JOSEF ŠKVORECKÝ, *The Engineer of Human Souls.*

GILBERT SORRENTINO, *Aberration of Starlight.*
Blue Pastoral.
Crystal Vision.

Imaginative Qualities of Actual Things.
Mulligan Stew. *Red the Fiend.*
Steelwork.
Under the Shadow.

MARKO SOSIČ, *Ballerina, Ballerina.*

ANDRZEJ STASIUK, *Dukla.*
Fado.

GERTRUDE STEIN, *The Making of Americans.*
A Novel of Thank You.

LARS SVENDSEN, *A Philosophy of Evil.*

PIOTR SZEWC, *Annihilation.*

GONÇALO M. TAVARES, *A Man: Klaus Klump.*
Jerusalem.
Learning to Pray in the Age of Technique.

LUCIAN DAN TEODOROVICI, *Our Circus Presents...*

NIKANOR TERATOLOGEN, *Assisted Living.*

STEFAN THEMERSON, *Hobson's Island.*
The Mystery of the Sardine.
Tom Harris.

TAEKO TOMIOKA, *Building Waves.*

JOHN TOOMEY, *Sleepwalker.*

DUMITRU TSEPENEAG, *Hotel Europa.*
The Necessary Marriage.
Pigeon Post.
Vain Art of the Fugue.

ESTHER TUSQUETS, *Stranded.*

DUBRAVKA UGRESIC, *Lend Me Your Character.*
Thank You for Not Reading.

TOR ULVEN, *Replacement.*

MATI UNT, *Brecht at Night.*
Diary of a Blood Donor.
Things in the Night.

ÁLVARO URIBE & OLIVIA SEARS, EDS., *Best of Contemporary Mexican Fiction.*

ELOY URROZ, *Friction.*
The Obstacles.

LUISA VALENZUELA, *Dark Desires and the Others.*
He Who Searches.

PAUL VERHAEGHEN, *Omega Minor.*

BORIS VIAN, *Heartsnatcher.*

FOR A FULL LIST OF PUBLICATIONS, VISIT: www.dalkeyarchive.com

LLORENÇ VILLALONGA, *The Dolls'*
Room.

TOOMAS VINT, *An Unending Landscape.*

ORNELA VORPSI, *The Country Where No*
One Ever Dies.

AUSTRYN WAINHOUSE, *Hedyphagetica.*

CURTIS WHITE, *America's Magic*
Mountain.
The Idea of Home.
Memories of My Father Watching TV.
Requiem.

DIANE WILLIAMS,
Excitability: Selected Stories.
Romancer Erector.

DOUGLAS WOOLF, *Wall to Wall.*
Ya! & John-Juan.

JAY WRIGHT, *Polynomials and Pollen.*
The Presentable Art of Reading Absence.

PHILIP WYLIE, *Generation of Vipers.*

MARGUERITE YOUNG, *Angel in the*
Forest.
Miss MacIntosh, My Darling.

REYOUNG, *Unbabbling.*

VLADO ŽABOT, *The Succubus.*

ZORAN ŽIVKOVIĆ , *Hidden Camera.*

LOUIS ZUKOFSKY, *Collected Fiction.*

VITOMIL ZUPAN, *Minuet for Guitar.*

SCOTT ZWIREN, *God Head.*

AND MORE . . .

9 781628 972740